Daybreak Sky

Daybreak Sky

Sky

sean hunter

A Novel

Daybreak Sky by Sean Hunter

© 2017 Sean Hunter

Cover by Sean Hunter

Thank you to the one who gives me happiness every day. With you, I know there will be love in my life wherever we may be in the world. Thank you to my parents for supporting me in all I've put them through. Thank you to those who pushed me to keep writing over the years.

Chapter 1

Once or twice a summer, he would rise before the sun and ride his bike to the ocean. Along the way he would stop and buy a doughnut and a bottle of orange juice. He would sit on the seawall and eat his breakfast and stare out over the ocean. If he could, he would do this every day, but he lacked the discipline. Instead he would wait until later in the day, brave the people and slow-driving tourists, and ride down to an out of the way turn-off that looked over the harbor.

The riding would be coming to an end soon. He was preparing to leave. Summer was winding down. He was going to a nearby city for school. Only a matter of weeks stood between him and the freedom he had been longing after for years. While he was nervous, he knew it would be better. Anything would have to be. All teenagers are anxious to escape their parents, he knew, but he especially was. The idea of the city seemed so new and bright and different. Unconfined. Mainly, it was away from his parents. Though the city wasn't that far, he knew they wouldn't come to visit too often. They simply weren't that affectionate.

Chapter 2

The time came and he was packed and he moved and he unpacked and there he was. He didn't have too much time to ponder the new state of things before he was thrown into orientation rituals and dragged out with his new roommates. As they traipsed about the city one night, they stumbled across the harbor. He paused by the edge and silently gazed over the quietly shifting dark mass. The city lights reflected amongst the boats and slowly moved back and forth.

"C'mon, man, we're going. We need to catch the last train."

He turned and followed and inside his chest he missed the ocean. It was a deep ache, but quickly lost in everything else. Soon enough he had classes and a part-time job and only worried about getting enough sleep and finding time to eat. He made friends with his roommates and a few kids on his floor. A girl who lived down the hall attracted his interested and he spent time with her whenever she was around.

People were much friendlier than they had been in high school. Mostly he would eat by himself, but often he wasn't allowed to.

"Hey."

He put his forkful of chicken and mashed potatoes back down on the tray and looked away from the TV.

"Hey."

"I'm Brian."

"Josh."

"Tell me about yourself."

He heard this a lot those first few months.

"There's nothing all that exciting to tell. I'm from a small town not too far from here. I played sports, did well in my classes. I've always been into art and that's what I want to do. I've got an internship at a design firm for the school year, actually, and I've got some freelance work."

The boy across the table persisted. "No, what do you like doing? What are you all about?"

"I don't know. I've got to get to class." He got up and walked to the exit of the dining hall, dropping his tray of mostly uneaten food off on his way out.

He liked art. That's what he did. What else was he supposed to say? He went to classes, he went to work, and he painted and drew. What else was there? He resolutely decided to figure out another activity to list for the next time he was asked this.

He didn't really have to go to class and had a few hours before he did. He wasn't up for dealing with his roommates so he decided to go for a walk. Everywhere he went there were people. He just wanted to be alone. At home there had been the woods and the beach and ample solitude.

He walked and walked, feeling more and more confined by the minute by the onslaughts of people. There was a park nearby and he went there thinking he could find a quiet space. There was none. He finally settled on a spot equidistant from a couple making out and a middle-aged woman meditating. He put his book bag down for a headrest and lay back. The sky wasn't particularly beautiful. It was in fact rather gray and overcast, quite typical of that time of year. It didn't matter to him. It was something other than the city and its people. He stared at it, working on calming himself. Finally he was ready to go.

As he was collecting his bag, he heard his name called.

"Josh! What are you up to tonight?"

It was one of the guys on his floor. "Nothing yet."

"A bunch of us are going to see a movie. Want to come?"

"Yeah, sure. Come by and get me before you go."

Chapter 3

As the months passed, he became accustomed to not having his own space. No matter where he went, there were people. He learned to find solitude even in the masses.

Winter began to set in and classes would be ending for the semester soon. The girl down the hall would be leaving to study abroad so they broke things off. Josh began to mentally prepare himself for going home. He had no choice because the dormitories would be closing. If he had lost his mental toughness he knew that it would be an awful break. He worried that the time away had made him too soft. He convinced his parents to drive him to the train every day so that he could go to his internship. Without that guaranteed break 5 days a week, he feared he wouldn't make it through the month.

He said good-bye to the girl and they agreed to stay friends and write while she was away. His things were packed and his parents came and loaded them into the car. He stared out the window at the sky as they drove him back to his hometown. They tried to ask him about classes and work, but after he gave his perfunctory answers, they fell silent.

He worked late most days and had his friends from home pick him up after so they could go out. The rare days that he had to be home he made a point of sequestering himself in his room in the evenings. His parents complained about the lack of time they got to spend with him, but he was unfazed. Preserving his sanity was all he cared about.

Christmas rolled around. It was the same routine as usual. Walk down the stairs as pictures were taken and make sure to smile. Stockings were opened first, then presents from relatives. Breakfast after they were done. After breakfast, off to the grandparents' house to see all the aunts and uncles and cousins. Hide outside or in the basement until it was time to cajole his parents into driving home before they were unable to. It never changed and it wore him down. He couldn't wait to be back at school and away from this. His dread of the upcoming summer intensified.

Break was finally over. His parents drove him back and he settled into his new classes. Soon enough he forgot about the break and refused to allow himself to think of the upcoming summer.

He didn't go out as much that semester. He focused on work and school and in his free time he simply rested. This trend stuck with him. By the end of his time at school he had only one or two good friends and a number of acquaintances he saw in passing.

That summer he returned to his hometown. He had a part-time job at an ice cream shop and much too much free time. The ocean beckoned to him again. He got himself up early at least once a week to go watch the sun rise up over the ocean. It helped him center himself better than anything else could. Mid-afternoon would find him at the spot by the harbor. Some evenings he would go to the beach once it was closed. He would watch the stars and listen to the sea. Sometimes he would take a girl he had met to sit with him on the seawall. He would hold her hand and look out over the water.

"What do you want to do?"

"Do you not like this?"

"It's nice and all, but it's a little boring. We do it all the time."

"Sorry. It's just so peaceful. It's so-- Never mind, we can go."

They got back into the car and drove circles around the town.

"I'm sorry, Josh. I just find it a little boring. I've seen it my whole life."

"Yeah, I know. I'm sorry. I couldn't think of anything else to do."

He hadn't tried to. He had assumed that she enjoyed the ocean too.

At the end of the summer they said good-bye. She went to school several hours away and neither would have a car. Things had faded after than night at the seawall and he didn't want to make an effort with her any longer.

Back at school, Josh made an effort to date. He had developed an intense loneliness while he had been at home and he longed to fill it. The girls he met did help, but he never felt close to any of them. He focused on his classes and put more time into his new internship. He wanted to succeed at his art more than anything now because he knew it could fill the hole. He would just have to wait patiently.

The internship turned into a part-time job that more than paid the bills. He never went home again for more than a few days after that. He had moved into an apartment and had no need to. This took a huge burden off of him, though all the anxiety compounded for the day visits instead of spreading over the month visits now.

He fell into a routine of working all day, coming home, eating dinner, and watching TV until he went to sleep. There was a comfort in the predictability. When school was in session, it was the same thing, with homework replacing TV. His last two years of school passed like this. His portfolio grew to include several large clients and he suspected finding work would be easy down the road.

Soon enough his school days began to draw to a close. He lined up a job at a company in the city, found a nicer apartment, and set about putting things in order.

Chapter 4

He graduated with honors and his parents came to watch. They were quite proud of him and took him out to dinner before leaving. They promised him a new bicycle as a present. This excited him as he had not had one in his four years of school and he had outgrown his old one. He had wanted one, but was hesitant to spend his savings, knowing the amount of debt he was graduating into.

They made plans to meet the next weekend so they could help him move and purchase the bike he was to pick out over the next few days. He returned to his room and packed up his undergraduate career.

He searched a number of bike shops and test rode a range of bikes. He initially wanted a road bike so he could get around the city quicker, but after a few rides on the pockmarked streets, he changed his mind. He found a bike that was affordable, but also durable enough to survive city streets and mountain trails. That weekend his parents loaded his things into the car, unloaded them, and drove to the bike store. They paid for the bike and he rode it to his new home. He didn't see them again for many months.

He returned to the new apartment and surveyed his room and piles of boxes. Mentally he arranged everything, then set about putting it in order. He finished half of it, gave up for the day, and walked out to the front porch. The view made him exceedingly happy. He could look over the city while being removed from it. His apartment was in a quiet neighborhood. There was even a wooded patch behind his house. When he woke up in the morning all he could see was trees outside of his windows. It was easy to forget where he was. On weekends when he had the luxury of sleeping late, he would watch the shadows play across his walls.

There was a large park nearby with dirt trails through its hills that he soon discovered. He would go here when he could. If he went early enough he wouldn't see any other people and it reminded him of home. He missed his old house and the yard and the quiet. The people he did not miss. Anytime he thought about it, he was thankful to have escaped. He debated going home for Thanksgiving as a perfunctory gesture, but found out his parents would not be there. He was grateful for not having to decide.

Every morning and every afternoon Josh would ride to and from work. Though there were many people and cars, he enjoyed it. He played games with them and turned it into a challenge, dodging and weaving around them, avoiding potholes and getting run over. Work was going well and he had been promoted out of his cubicle and into an office. This gave him privacy to change clothes so he didn't worry about pushing himself and getting sweaty.

Soon he began to feel unsure about what to do with all the free time the lack of classes left him. He would go on longer rides a couple times a week and begun to pick up other hobbies. He briefly took an interest in crafting things and built himself a paper lantern. A few months later he saw a flyer on a bulletin board for something called dragon boating. He had no idea what this was, but he knew in involved being on the water.

He joined late in the season and felt out of place. This he got over quickly as he paddled down the river. The smell of the water sated something in him. He didn't care how wet or tired he got, all he wanted was that *smell*. He contentedly finished out the season, paddling until it got much too cold.

That winter he found no new hobbies. It got too cold to ride his bike to work. Restlessness became pervasive. He began dating again and reading feverishly to fill the time. He enjoyed the company of his various dates, but lacked interest in pursuing any of them.

The library more and more became his sanctuary. As a child he frequented the library several times a week. While other children would play outside, he would read. Each summer he set a goal of reading 100 books. The other children would read their school-mandated 5-10, but he took pleasure in surpassing his goal. It brought him great satisfaction to rediscover this childhood comfort.

At first he set about to read his usual--the classics. He liked being able to rattle off the impressive tomes to others. He had plenty of time to question the subject matter now. Gradually, he started to formulate his own answers and questions.

But, quickly, he became overwhelmed. Indeed, some of his questions were answered, but so many ones sprung up in their place. Uncertainty overtook him. Every book he read, every newspaper, every magazine gave him something new to think about. Much of the material contradicted other things he had read.

The power of this hit him. He did not know the truth. How could he know the truth? Where would it come from?

Chapter 5

In a coffee shop one day a girl struck up a conversation with him.

"*A People's History*? That's a great book. Do you like Zinn?"

"I haven't read anything else of his. But this is good so far."

"I love how he exposes this whole other side of history that no one hears about. They'd never teach this in school."

He paused. "Does it ever bother you that the truth is so elusive? Like, without reading a book like this you might never know the true facts. Or that this book might not even be true at all?"

She looked at him uncertainly. "Well, I guess if you want to know the truth about something you just have to read all you can and figure it out yourself."

He jumped. "But that's just it! We all formulate our own truths. How do we ever know which one is in fact true?"

They went back and forth like this for a while. She seemed a little unsure of the proceedings. By the time he got around to asking her name and for a second meeting, though, she said yes. She had decided that his was a tortured philosophical artist's soul and wanted to know more.

They continued to see each other. Josh made a point of not talking about truth too often, for he knew that it wasn't really polite dinner conversation. Anna was grateful for this because she no longer knew what to say to him about it. She didn't question truth.

"Do you think there is such a thing as truth or that it's all relative? Like how people see God."

Wearily she answered, "Yes, I think that it's probably closer to it than the idea of one hard and fast truth."

Lately he had been bringing this up more. She had long since stopped thinking about it. She would answer with whatever she thought he wanted to hear.

"How do any of us agree on anything then?"

"Josh, I don't know. We just do. We have to in order to get by. Now turn off the light."

He did as she said. It had been about a year since they met. He was content in the relationship, but he could sense her frustration with him when he brought up topics like this. She didn't wonder about things like this, nor was she inclined to unless pushed. And the more he pushed, the less patient she became. He felt it was a matter of time before she left. But for now, he was making good money at work and supporting her to an extent. She wouldn't leave unless something drastic changed.

She was aware of a growing distance between them. Josh spoke to her less and less and spent more time with his books. She had yet to discover a way to bring his attention back to her, but she was determined to try.

Josh was reading through his books at a tremendous pace. But he was disheartened because he still had no answers. After much contemplation he came to the conclusion that his present situation wouldn't do. The routine of work and reading and spending time with Anna had provided him no insights. His time was filled, but he was restless. He longed for an adventure. Anything that would challenge him. This he was sure would get his mind working and processing again.

Chapter 6

It was spring and the thoughts of change grew stronger. This time of year always brought the need to start fresh to a head in him. Those first few days when he could actually smell spring were exhilarating to him.

His sense of adventure was at a high. As he rode to work one day he knew suddenly what it was he wanted to do.

Before bed that night, he broached the subject Anna. "Anna, we should talk. I've been doing some thinking."

"Um...ok. Go ahead."

"Well, I want to go for a bike ride."

"What? That's it? Isn't it a little late?" She had been expecting to hear much worse.

"No, no. I don't mean now."

"Well, when?"

"Soon. As soon as I can. I have plenty of vacation time. I haven't used any."

"Wait, what do you need to use vacation time for?"

"I want to ride down the coast," Josh said matter-of-factly.

Her eyes widened. "Do you know how far that is? That's several hundred miles, at least."

"I know, but it's something I need to do. I'm going to take two weeks and then fly back."

Anna didn't say a word. She didn't even know where to start. He stared at her with his head slightly cocked to the side. He moved to speak, but checked himself and waited.

She broke the silence. "What... What is wrong with you? Where is this coming from? All the reading and moping around and distance and...everything! Now this crazy idea! What is all of this?"

He mournfully looked at her, not wanting to answer.

"I don't know."

"You don't know? You're going to go on this crazy bike ride and you can't even tell me why?"

"I'm restless."

He looked so sad and pathetic she didn't want to continue, but she was baffled.

"Go to the gym. Go for a ride around the city. Take up a sport! Restless..."

He desperately wanted to explain. He didn't know how. It was a feeling that he had no words for. He felt himself shutting down. He was simply overwhelmed and he was retreating into himself.

"Well, it's that..." He hesitated. "I don't know what to do with myself. I don't like my life right now. I'm not happy."

She sat up straight. "Is this your weird way of breaking up with me? Because, really, there are better ways to do it."

"Huh? No, not at all. That's not it. I'm not unhappy with you."

At this point he about gave up on conversing. "We'll talk tomorrow, ok? We both need some time to think it over." With that he rolled over. She stared at his back for hours before calming down enough to do the same.

He arranged for his vacation time at work. It was a month away so he busily prepared. Every day he rode further and longer. He acquired panniers, a good lightweight pack, a sleeping bag, and the appropriate clothes and shoes. He took a bicycle repair class. A reliable camera was purchased, along with many rolls of film. In preparation for all the insightful thoughts he was preparing to have, he packed a notebook and plenty of pens.

The day arrived. He awoke early and watched the shadows float across the walls. Anna was still asleep next to him. She lie there, looking content, her mouth open slightly. The sun brushed her face, illuminating the right side and lighting up the tips of her eyelashes. The light turned her skin to a pure white and she was simply beautiful. He would miss her, he thought to himself. When he got back he knew things would be different between them. She wasn't happy about all of this.

Through the trees he could see the sky outside his window. It was clear blue. Slowly he sat up and carefully crawled over Anna and off the bed.

The bike sat in the hall and quickly he loaded up the last of his things. He decided to take a shower before he left, not knowing when he'd next have that chance.

By the time he emerged, Anna had woken. She made her way to him as he got dressed.

"You're really going through with this?"

"I need to."

Her face scrunched up. "You'll call, right?"

"Of course. And two weeks isn't that long."

They hugged and he left. He was nervous and not sure if he was ready, but he felt that it was the right thing to do.

He had yet to ride through the city this early in the day on the weekend. Everything was so fresh. The sporadic patches of grass were still wet. The sunlight was golden and there was a faint early-morning haze. No one else was out. It was startling how quiet and still it was.

He paused briefly to look over the rest of the city. Josh smiled to himself and knew that this would be good. Off he went.

A few miles into his ride it occurred to him that he would pass by his parents' house. He debated stopping. He hadn't spoken to them in months. Finally he decided that he wasn't going to pass up a break and a good meal. And it was still early in the day so it wouldn't be so bad.

He rode on and further away from his home. There was an increasing awareness of his distance from his space. He was moving outside his comfort zone. He felt a little thrill at this. Never had he done anything like this. Soon, perhaps, things would all start making sense to him.

He crossed into his hometown. A few more miles and his parents' house was visible down the street. At the driveway he got off the bike and walked it around to the back. Not surprisingly, his parents were both sitting on the porch as per their usual weekend routine.

His dad called to him, "Hey Josh. What are you doing here?"

"Did you ride all the way here?" his mom asked.

"Hi mom. Hi dad. Yeah, I rode here. I'm planning on going for a pretty long ride."

"How long? Not much further than this, I hope."

"Actually, dad, I'm riding down the coast."

Neither of them said a word.

His mom asked him with a hint of concern in her voice, "What about work? You still have a job, right?"

"Yeah, I'm just taking some vacation time. No big deal. I have a lot I haven't used."

"Oh, ok. That's good."

"Do you really think this is a good idea?" His dad was frowning. "I don't think you're up for it."

"Dad, I just wanted to stop by and let you know that I'll be gone. I'm not going to argue this with you."

"It's dangerous. You might get hurt and who's even going to know?"

"I told Anna I'll call her. If she doesn't hear from me she'll call someone. I'm not talking about this anymore."

He regretted coming already. Nothing ever changed with them. He was glad he hadn't come later in the day, knowing how much worse it would be. He made a sandwich, promised them he'd call at least once, and said good-bye.

He decided to ride down by the harbor before he continued on. Sitting on the rocks overlooking the harbor, he felt much calmer. A familiar sense of peace filled him. But there was something else there. He realized that he felt a nagging sense of being trapped. It was as though being here and interacting with his parents had brought him back to that place that he used to inhabit many years ago. This surprised him, feeling all those emotions coming back. He thought that by moving away and being on his own he had escaped them. He was perturbed. His peace was invaded by these unwelcome feelings. He wouldn't go back to that place. It was time to go.

He rode away quickly. After about 20 minutes he stopped on the side of the road. Josh knew better than to ride that hard for a ride like this. He forced himself to pause and take a breath. Riding in this state of mind would accomplish nothing. Why had he gone there? He knew full well how it always messed with his head. He always hoped it would be different, but that was never the case. This wasn't the start he was looking for.

The strip mall to his right seemed to mock him. Its soulless promises of finding satisfaction in its wares. The illusion of greatness hiding something empty. He wearily walked through the parking lots toward the stores. All he wanted was to go back to his apartment and hide. It was too soon to go back, though. He was not one to back down and he refused to concede defeat on this. He paused in front of a dollar store. His eyes ran over the trinkets in the window. No, he had to go on. He had to move past this. There had to be more than this out there.

He got back on his bike, surveyed the road ahead, and set back out with a much better mindset. As the sun started setting he kept an eye out for a place to sleep. He spotted a town green with a fair number of trees and pulled over there. He locked his bike to a tree and grabbed a sandwich out of his pack. He contentedly ate and watched the traffic patterns around the green. Darkness came and the streetlights came on.

It pleased him to find that his spot was in the shadows. With some luck, no one would bother him. The white and red lights moving along the outskirts of the grass became fewer.

Josh lay back on his sleeping bag and could see a handful of stars through the branches. It was nice to see stars again. There were so few visible through the lights of the city. Peacefully he fell asleep.

Morning came and he awoke grateful to have not been disturbed. His hand itched and he noticed a cluster of pink bumps dotting it. Annoyed that he hadn't bothered to set up his tent, he quickly rolled up his sleeping bag and packed. He was about to go explore the town center, but realized it was much too soon in his journey. He wouldn't get very far if he did that every day.

Off he went again. Soon, he warmed up enough so that muscles no longer ached. The state border appeared. As he crossed it, it felt as if the great unknown had finally opened up to him.

As unfamiliar territory passed by, he began to ponder things. The main question he had for himself was the hardest. What was he working towards? What did he want? He had known at one point. First, it was doing well in high school so that he could go to college. Then it was finding good internships and doing well in college so he could get a good job. But that was as far as things were planned. He had that job now. There were no more goals. What does everyone else do at this point, he wondered. There were no guides for him. People got married, bought houses, had kids. This didn't interest him, except for maybe the house, but he didn't think of that as a goal.

The sun had shifted to his right. It was time for lunch. His stomach grumbled angrily. With a quick look around he decided that there should be restaurants a few blocks over. All towns were basically laid out the same. He hoped to find a diner. Anything nicer probably wouldn't be too happy with him sitting to eat without changing first.

He stopped a pedestrian on the sidewalk. He was an older gentleman who looked like he would know his way around.

"Are there any diners around here?"

"No, but there is a quiet little café about three streets over. Where are you coming from?"

"Rossdale."

"All the way up there? What are you doing here?"

"Just going for a ride. Which way did you say the café is?"

"Go to the end of this street and take a right. Go three streets over. It's the only place to eat over there so you can't miss it."

"Alright. Thanks."

"Well, enjoy your ride."

"I will."

He pedaled down the street and made a right at the end. The café was five streets down, but he found it without much trouble. There was a rail to lock the bike to and he went inside. It was what he was looking for. The red and white checked tiled floor needed replacing decades ago. The same could be said for the blue- and white-flecked Formica tables. There were only two customers. An older man sat reading the day's paper and drinking coffee. A younger unshaven and rumpled man sat at the counter watching the news. Pleased with what he saw, Josh sat in a corner table and perused the menu.

"Can I getcha anything to drink?

"How about a coffee and some water."

"Sure thing. You look like you could use the coffee."

"Yeah, I've been riding for a day and a half. Takes a lot of out me."

"I'd guess so! I'll go get those for you."

She returned a few minutes later with the coffee and two glasses of water.

"Thought you might be thirsty," she grinned.

He looked up at her and smiled. She was in her late 20s and fairly attractive. There was life in her eyes that he was surprised to see. Most people he encountered in her position had eyes that betray their boredom and loathing for their job. He was intrigued.

"Thank you. So have you been working here long?"

"Since high school. It's not a bad job. Just a little slow sometimes. Do you want to order now?"

He ordered his meal and she disappeared into the back. He was curious, unsure of how she could still enjoy her job. It was such a lowly, thankless job, but she still had that life in her eyes. He had been at his job only a few years yet he could already sense that spark fading from his eyes. Everyone at his firm had the same dull look in their eyes. He wanted to escape that same fate, but he knew it was inevitable. Yet here was this woman who still had life in her eyes…

She arrived with his food and plunked it down in front of him.

"So why have you worked here so long? I'm sure you could find something else."

She gave him a funny look. "Why would I want to? I like it here. I like seeing new people and catching up with the regulars. I make enough to live on. What reason do I have for leaving?"

"I guess you don't. Can I get some more water?"

He finished his meal and paid the check at the counter. He left her a generous tip. Unlocking his bike, he puzzled over their conversation. She lacked ambition. This was so strange to him. That was all he had known.

Without it he had become lost. He was miserable and yet she was content. It made no sense.

Fifty more miles and the sky was darkening. His surroundings were more rural now so he didn't have to look long for a place to sleep. A wooded stretch extending off the side of the road provided all the cover he needed.

With a hint of disappointment, he noticed there were no stars tonight. The look of the clouds made him wary and he set up his small tent and put a tarp over his bike. He walked for a bit and found what he was looking for. He stripped down and crouched in the stream. Something deeper would have been preferable, but this would do. He washed the dirt and sweat from his skin and dipped his head into the crisp water to clean his hair. Satisfied, he swirled his clothes through the water. He picked them up and walked back to his tent, stark naked, but confident no one else would be around. He carefully hung the dripping clothes over some low branches, not wanting to wake up to damp, dirt-covered shorts and shirts. He could see the lights from the cars where he was, silent lights rushing by, first white, then red. "These will have to be my stars tonight," he mumbled sadly.

The waitress was still on his mind as he drifted to sleep. He wished he knew her name. He decided to call her Adelaide. When he was young, he had watched a house that belonged to an opera singer, Adelaide Phillips, burn to the ground. The fire and that name had stayed with him over the years, though he couldn't say why.

Chapter 7

The rain woke him up. He cursed to himself. "I guess my clothes will be extra clean," he muttered. The bike was only a few feet away so he darted over and grabbed his pack. He sat in the corner of his tent and wiped as much rainwater off his skin as he could with his hands, taking care to not dampen his sleeping bag. It wasn't cold, but he put on his warm clothes. The only others he had were nice and he wanted to keep them clean.

He fished a granola bar out of his bag and debated what to do. He could ride in the rain, it wouldn't bother him. But he was worried about his stuff getting too wet or maybe misjudging the unfamiliar road and having an accident. Wasting time would do him no good either. Two weeks wasn't that long and he had far to go still. Sighing, he took off his warm clothes. He packed them and his sleeping bag, then darted outside and donned his soaking clothes. The rest of his stuff was packed and he walked toward the road. There were no cars, so he slowly clipped in his left foot, pushed off, and fumbled to get his right foot clipped as well. He made his way substantially slower than the previous two days. Down the road he saw a glow and decided he should stop and call Anna.

He found a pay phone and dialed Anna's number. It rang 5 times and he hung up. On 6 the answering machine would kick in and he didn't want to waste his quarters. He tried his apartment, but again got no answer. He knew he owed his parents a phone call, but was not ready to talk to them again. They could wait.

The rain was now falling in sheets, hard enough that it bounced up about a foot after it hit. He could make out the blue neon glow of what he hoped was a diner down the street. He pulled up in front and didn't bother locking his bike. Anyone who would steal it in this weather was probably determined enough not to be deterred by a lock. He shook off as much as he could in the doorway and took a seat at a booth. No one else was there. The cook and the waitress stood leaning against the counter watching TV. She watched the soap opera for a few more minutes before coming over.

"You follow the soaps at all?"

"Can't say I do. I'm usually at work."

"You're not now."

"Nope, I'm on vacation."

"And you came here? This isn't much of a vacation."

"Actually, I'm riding my bike down the coast. This just happened to be one of the stops along the way."

"Huh." She looked at him suspiciously,

as if she couldn't believe anyone could be so foolish. "Well, what can I get you?'

"Water and coffee for now. I need a few more minutes."

She went back to the kitchen, but first stopped for a bit to watch TV.

When she brought his drinks he inquired, "Have you been working here long?"

"About a year now. It's just a temporary thing, you know? I sing at night. Once I save up enough I'm moving west."

"Oh, really? So you don't like it here?"

"Hell no! I'm getting out as soon as I can. It's dead around here."

"Yeah, it is. Can I get a burger?"

"Sure thing, hon."

She certainly didn't like her job. Clearly she just worked it for the paycheck. She wasn't at all like Adelaide.

After only a few minutes she returned with his burger. It must have been on the grill for hours. As he chewed the tough meat, he thought about the differences between Adelaide and this waitress. This one had a dream and a desire to go somewhere. How could she be happy in her present situation? Adelaide didn't want anything else and therefore she could find contentment, he supposed.

"Maybe that's it," he said quietly.

"Do you need something, hon?" the waitress called over.

His head jerked up. "Uh, yeah, some more water please?"

He finished his burger and went to pay the bill.

"Any coffee places around here?"

"There's one a couple miles down the road. It's called Java Joe. It'll be on your left."

"Thanks."

The rain hadn't let up any. It wasn't worth riding any further. He found the coffee place, got some tea, and went to a chair in the back corner. He dug through his pack and found his notebook and a pen. He had lost his train of thought from before, so he instead made a quick sketch of the coffee shop. Then he drew the woods and the stream from the previous night from memory.

Adelaide. That's what he had been thinking about. Quickly, he wrote, not wanting to lose it again.

Maybe there's happiness in not wanting. If I have no dreams and don't want anything, I can't be disappointed. I can't be impatient. There's nothing to be impatient about. There's nothing wrong with doing the same thing day in and day out and not wanting anything else. I would know myself so well because I wouldn't be distracted with trying to get ahead all the time. I could just live. What have I been fighting for anyhow? What was the point? What would it accomplish?

As he wrote a verse from the Tao Te Ching flitted through his mind.

The contentment one has when he knows he has enough
That is abiding contentment indeed

He had the answer all along, he just couldn't realize it. It took a waitress in a small town to show him.

"Thank you, Adelaide," he whispered.

He picked up his things and ran across the street to where he had seen a payphone.

It rang twice before she answered.

"Anna!"

"What? What's wrong Josh?"

"Nothing's wrong. I've found what I was looking for. I can't wait to see you again. I've got so much thinking to do, but I've figured out what about. This is all worth it."

"I should hope so."

"I miss you."

"I miss you too. Come home soon."

"I will, just another week and a half. I'll give you a call in a few more days."

"Ok, be safe. Bye."

"I will. Bye."

He turned and looked up into the sky. The clouds had lightened a bit. The day was a waste as far as riding, but he didn't care. He felt rejuvenated. He retrieved his bike and set off again. The rain pelted against his face. Twenty slow miles later he turned down a fire road. He walked his bike up a small hill. Sleeping in a low area would mean waking up in a puddle. Hunger cramped up his stomach, but he wasn't about to go out in the rain again. Some trail mix and a granola bar would do.

Josh lay down and debated what to do. Perhaps he'd just stop worrying about promotions. There was nothing wrong with his current job. He didn't have as much creative freedom as he wanted, but he wasn't doing the tedious grunt work of assembling other people's work. While he could live without promotions, it would only be acceptable as long as his current position didn't embarrass him. He couldn't have his friends from work looking down on him. As an afterthought, he decided to not purchase any more unnecessary luxury items. Possibly he would get rid of some of the ones he had now. Satisfied with these decisions, he allowed himself to sleep.

Chapter 8

He awoke with the sun the next morning. Not riding most of the day before had left him with an excess of energy. He stepped out of the tent. The sun was just peeking over the horizon. The trees were still dripping slowly, but in a few hours everything would be dry again.

From his panniers he removed a dry pair of shoes. The wet ones he tied on top. Packed, he walked to the end of the fire road and rode off.

Not wanting to waste any of the day, he stopped at a fast food restaurant for breakfast. He hoped to push himself and ride 100 miles. He finished his breakfast and got back on the bike, riding slowly with coffee in hand.

He rode hard that day and got in 93 miles. The sun was setting, but he couldn't find anywhere to sleep. The area had become more urban. He decided to treat himself to a hotel. A hot shower and real bed would do him good. He ate in the hotel restaurant and watched the TV over the bar. The waitress looked harried so he didn't try to strike up a conversation. There was no need to, he had his answer. The local news was on. The standard stories of political scandals and the state of the economy were hyped. He lost interest. He finished his meal and wandered into the lobby.

There was a lone payphone. He dropped his quarters in and was about to call his parents when he realized the time. It was 8:30. He couldn't call. Instead he called Anna. He would talk to them in the morning. She answered on the third ring.

"Hi, honey. How are you?"

"I'm ok. How's your ride going?"

"Good. It poured yesterday, but it's been good. I'm feeling a lot better about things."

"Yeah, you seemed pretty excited yesterday. What happened?"

"I sort of had a personal breakthrough. I'll talk to you more about it when I get back."

"Ok, sweetie. I'm going to go, ok? My show's on."

"That's fine. I'll call again in a few days."

"Bye."

"Bye."

Slowly he walked over to the elevator. His room was on the second floor, but he was sore. A long bath temporarily relieved that.

It was still dark when he woke. Something didn't feel right, though. He looked to the windows and realized the blinds were drawn. Quickly he looked at the clock. 2:00. He jumped out of bed.

"Wake up call. Should have had a wake up call." Half the day was wasted. He threw on his clothes, grabbed his bike and headed for the elevator. His legs ached unmercifully. He checked out and found out he was charged an extra day because it was after 11. This, along with his frustration and pain caused him to get progressively angrier. He threw caution to the wind and decided to call his parents. It couldn't make things worse.

He walked over to the payphone in the lobby.

It rang four times. The answering machine picked up and he was grateful to not have to talk to them.

"Hi mom and dad. Just calling to check in and l-" He heard a click.

"Hi Josh. How are you?"

"Hi mom. I'm fine. I was just calling to let you know I'm alright."

"That's great. How's your ride so far?"

"It's good. I'm having a good time."

"That's good. You know, you left so fast the other day we forgot to tell you our news."

"What news?"

"We're moving!"

"You're what?"

"Moving to Florida."

"You're kidding, right?"

"Nope, we're putting the house on the market next week."

"Oh. Well. That's great…"

He was taken aback by all of this. They had never mentioned even thinking about moving.

"Are you guys retiring or did you find new jobs?"

"Oh, we're retiring. We think we've earned it by now."

"Ok."

"You don't sound too happy."

"I'm just a little surprised, that's all. But good for you. I'm happy for you."

The operator cut in, requesting more money. He used the interruption to end the call.

"Well, I'm out of money, mom. I've got to go. I'll call in a few days. Say hi to dad."

"I will. Have a good trip."

"Thanks, bye."

He hung up and stood looking at the phone for a minute.

"Sir, are you done?"

"Uh…yeah. Sorry." He hadn't noticed the woman waiting. He reached for his bike that was leaning against the wall and walked toward the door. Confusion overwhelmed him. He wasn't sure how to feel. His parents and he were not on good terms, but he was used to having them around. It would be weird not having them nearby. It would be weird to have strangers living in his childhood house.

It was getting to be late afternoon. He hoped for 30 or 40 miles of riding before nightfall. He ate a granola bar as he rode.

Them moving would remove a huge

source of stress from his life, he supposed. A yearly visit and an occasional phone call would be his only obligations. He would be able to better focus on his life with them further away.

He had traveled into a more suburban area again and was thankful for this. He wasn't quite sure where he was, but he realized that he could smell the ocean. He hadn't realized he was so close to the coast. Deciding that he was pretty much done riding for the day, he swung eastwards. The ocean was only two streets over. He locked his bike to the guardrail and took off his shoes. There were a handful of people on the beach, but not enough to bother him. He strode down to the water, rolled up his pants and waded in. The water was icy. His toes began to numb. He scurried back out. He stood at the edge of the water, allowing it to touch his toes when it rushed in far enough. He watched the darkness creep up over the horizon as the sun set behind him. Finally he turned and walked back to the bike, not wanting to wait until darkness was complete before finding somewhere to sleep.

He was pleased to note that there was none of the same fear as the last time he was at the ocean. The closeness of his parents must have been the cause the last time, he surmised. He was glad they hadn't been able to take the ocean from him too.

He rode through the town and made note of a park with a good number of trees. If he didn't pitch his tent no one would notice him there. He kept riding until he reached a sub shop. Nothing fancy tonight. He put his sandwich into his pack and rode back to the park. He spread his sleeping bag, sat, and ate.

They were leaving. This knowledge freed something inside of him. Their absence would open up so much for him. He didn't know what, but he knew this would be the case. As he lay down to go to sleep he wondered who would buy the house.

Morning came and he awoke with a start, realizing that he was wet. He was worried for a moment that it had rained. This was not the case. Instead, he was covered with a heavy dew. He sighed, shook off his bag, and packed it up. He stopped by a coffee shop, got a doughnut and coffee, ate hurriedly and went on his way. Almost a week had passed. Having found his answer, he had no reason to continue, but he was enjoying the break from everything. This had been a productive trip. Perhaps he'd do it again.

Settling into a moderate pace, he traveled down the road. Another 50 miles and he would take a break. Passing by a rather picturesque area, he realized he had yet to take any pictures or even write much. Something like this deserved to be better documented. He pulled off to the side of the road and dug out his camera. He took a couple pictures and slung it around his neck. Getting back on the bike, he resolved to stop more often to take pictures and maybe jot some notes down.

He swung eastwards, wanting to ride by the water again. Some pictures would be nice too. The town he was riding through reminded him of his hometown. He felt vaguely nostalgic. He reached a seawall and sat down. He missed his early morning rides to the ocean and his mid-afternoon rides to the harbor and his evening rides to watch the stars over the water.

He looked up with a start. There was a solution to that yearning.

"I can go back," he said aloud.

A couple passers-by looked at him, but he paid them no heed.

He stood up and said excitedly, "I could go back!"

His parents were moving. Their house would be for sale. He could buy it. He could go back.

Everything began to fall into place. What better way to simplify his life? He'd have no desire to outdo anyone there. That competitive edge was largely absent. People just went about their business. No one would be pressuring him. He'd be on completely familiar ground.

He was pacing back and forth along the seawall, quietly muttering to himself. People had moved away slightly.

There was a better answer to forgoing

promotions, he realized. He would quit his job. Why participate in that world at all? He could do anything. He was sure he could find a job close to the house. There would be no need to commute. He'd have his ocean, he'd have his space. His parents would be gone. He was ecstatic.

He took some pictures to remember this place. This place led to this breakthrough and he didn't want to ever forget it. Suddenly he realized he was pacing and noticed his surroundings again. People were looking at him. He shouldered his pack and rode away.

This new realization increased his contentment. He rode quietly for a bit, just enjoying the surroundings. He debated when to call his parents. Then he remembered what his mother said. The house would be on the market in a few days. He looked at his watch and decided it might still be early enough. He pulled into a general store a couple miles down the road to use the payphone.

It rang twice and a groggy voice answered. He instantly wanted to hang up, but a sense of urgency kept him on the line.

"Hi mom. I just wanted to talk to you quickly."

"What do you want?"

"I want to buy the house."

"Shut up. What do you want?"

"No, really, I want to buy the house."

"Wait. Who is this?"

"It's your son Josh, mom."

"Josh, how are you? Why don't you ever call? You're a bad son."

"I talked to you yesterday."

"Noooo, you didn't."

"Listen I'll talk to you tomorrow, ok?"

"You never talk to me. You don't love me."

"Bye, mom," he said firmly. He hung up.

He was disappointed with himself. He knew better. It had been too late.

He rode hard and fast, seeking to quell the rising emotions. One call and all those memories came flooding back. He hated how vulnerable he was to them. Why couldn't he shake this? It followed him, always lurking somewhere in his mind, just waiting to surface. He wondered if he'd ever be able to shake it.

After just a few miles he was exhausted. He sat up straight to try to catch his breath. His anger had been replaced with a huge sense of emptiness. He hated them for this.

Wearily, he got off his bike and walked it to a bench nearby. He let the bike fall to the ground and sat down. He sat, head hanging between his knees, feeling all of his former teenage angst come fighting back to the surface. He hated them. He hated himself. He hated this unshakable pain.

He understood then that he did have to move to that house. He had to for all the same reasons. But he also had to because it would be the only way to fight their lingering demons. It was a fight he could never win with them. So many times before he had fought it. Once, maybe twice, they promised change and he felt triumphant. It was always so hollow, though. It was just a matter of days before things reverted back. Aside from that, they never tried. They never even admitted wrongdoing. If he couldn't fight them and win, perhaps he'd fare better fighting with their memories. He had to try. He was desperate to escape this. He couldn't let them continue to do this.

He sat staring straight ahead, letting all his emotions seep off. A few deep breaths and he felt ready to continue.

It would be nightfall in an hour. He felt drained and didn't want to continue today. A nice dinner would cheer him up, he decided. He used a gas station bathroom to change into his nice clothes that he had been saving. There had been a respectable looking restaurant a short way back that he decided to go to. Not caring how he looked, he rolled up the right pant leg of his slacks. It wouldn't do to get them caught in the chain or covered in its grease. He pedaled carefully and slowly down the street.

The restaurant parking lot was relatively empty, which made him happy. He locked his bike to the wooden fence and went inside to wait to be seated. It took only as long as it took the hostess to grab the menu. She seated him in a booth by the window. Usually he ate fairly carefully so that he'd have the energy for riding, but he didn't have the motivation. He knew full well that he was eating in an attempt to sooth his earlier pain, but he didn't stop himself. All he wanted was the temporary relief it would provide.

He shrugged the consequences off, choosing to be sated now and miserable tomorrow. Nachos laden with beef, beans, cheese, jalapenos, olives, salsa, sour cream, and guacamole were first on the list. That was followed by fettuccini Alfredo with plenty of garlic bread. To finish things off he had a large ice cream sundae, replete with brownie, nuts, whipped cream and a cherry. He ate it all, despite the fullness of his stomach. Even as pain and nausea overtook his strained stomach, he felt better. The food filled the emptiness and forced out the pain. There was literally no room for it.

The food provided him with the high he needed. Already he felt guilty and berated himself for his actions, but he was satisfied.

He rode slowly now, not out of care, but because he could do nothing else. With exhaustion rapidly overtaking him, he made his way to a stretch of woods that separated the road he was on from the highway. It was noisy, but he couldn't bring himself to go further. His stomach was shifting and grumbling and he needed to lie down. Not caring if he could be seen, he stripped down and climbed into his sleeping bag. The fleece lining was comforting to his skin and he quickly fell asleep.

Chapter 9

The sounds of rush hour traffic woke him. The highway was closer than he thought. He was probably visible to anyone who bothered to look out his or her car window. Not wanting to be seen unclothed, he rolled in his sleeping bag over to where his pack lay in the dirt. He fished around for his shorts, retrieved them, and pulled them on. Then he finally emerged from the sleeping bag. His stomach still grumbled unhappily and he knew he would not be able to ride far today. He finished getting dressed and packed up his gear. As he did so he saw his camera.

This brought back memories of the previous day at the beach and the conversation with his mother. He realized that she would not remember it and would still be planning on putting the house up for sale. Hastily he decided it was time to go back. He rode back towards town and stopped the first person he saw.

"Where's the nearest airport?"

"Well, I guess that would be Dighton International. It's about 30 miles south of here. It's right outside of the city."

"Thanks."

He headed south, moving along at a

good clip. His stomach cramped quickly, but he ignored it and pushed on. His legs cramped next. He forced himself on, ignoring the burning as best he could, but he was forced to drop the pace several notches. This displeased him, but his body refused to work any harder.

As he neared Dighton he passed a sign for a bike shop. Realizing that he would need to ship his bike back, he took a sharp left. He found the store and arranged to return it soon and left a sizeable deposit. With any luck the bike would arrive a day or two after he did.

They let him use their phone and he called for a cab. He browsed around the store looking at all the newest gear until he heard a honk outside. He walked out and got into the cab.

"Airport," was all he said and the taxi pulled away.

Josh couldn't remember the last time he had been in a car. He thought it might have been when he had moved into his apartment. He felt so disconnected riding in the confined space as cars and trees blurred by. When he rode on his bike he was connected to his surroundings. He was an active participant. It was necessary to his survival that he was. He was used to seeing cars as obstacles, at best, and enemies, at worst. They hurtled towards the airport. He stared mindlessly out the window and entrusted the remainder of his journey to the cab driver.

"Which terminal?"

"Any one is fine. Any domestic."

The driver slammed to a stop in front of the next set of doors.

"This is fine, thanks."

He grabbed his pack and his panniers, paid the driver, and climbed out.

He walked to the ticket counter line. The airport was crowded and he felt out of place. He hadn't thought to change out of his cycling clothes when he had time at the bike store. He felt conspicuous. The line moved slowly, but finally it was his turn.

"Hi, I need a one-way ticket to Rossdale."

"Leaving when, sir?"

"As soon as possible."

The lady behind the counter eyed him suspiciously. He should have changed. "One-way, you said?"

"Yes. You see, I rode my bike here from Rossdale."

As soon as he said that he regretted it. She furrowed her brow. He knew it sounded crazy.

He decided to lie and continued, "I was going to keep riding, but I just found out that my mother's really sick and I need to get back right away to see her. That's why I'm dressed like this."

Her face softened a bit and he mentally sighed with relief.

"The next flight leaves in 45 minutes. I can get you a seat on that. It's non-stop."

"That's great. I really appreciate it." He paid for the ticket, collected his things, and headed for the nearest restroom. He changed into his nice clothes in a stall and took a few minutes to clean up at the sink. He didn't feel like attracting any more attention.

He heard the boarding announcement and hurried to the gate.

The flight back was uneventful. A few hours later and a week's worth of southward riding was erased. He disembarked and walked to the bank of payphones.

"Hi, Anna."

"Josh! How are you? How's your trip going?"

"I'm good. I'm back in Rossdale. I'll be home in half an hour."

"You're here? What happened? Why are you back?"

"Don't worry, nothing's wrong. I'll tell you all about it when I see you. I'll see you soon."

"Ok. I love you."

"I love you too."

He followed the crowds to baggage, realized he still had his pack and panniers with him, and walked outside. Twenty minutes went by and finally the shuttle bus appeared. Anna expected him home in five minutes. Not wanting to cause more problems than he knew he would be already, he skipped the bus and found his way to the taxi queue. He gave the driver his address and pointedly stared out the window, not feeling up for conversation.

He arrived in front of his apartment building. It had only been a week but it looked so unfamiliar to him. He paid and turned towards the house just as Anna opened the door.

"You're late."

"Aw, come on. Five minutes."

"I'm just teasing you. I missed you. Five minutes seemed long." She walked down the stairs and took the panniers from him.

"I missed you too. It's good to be back." He said this from force of habit. He didn't know yet if it was good to be back. He supposed that he wouldn't be here much longer so it didn't really matter.

They walked inside and he walked down the hall toward his room to begin unpacking.

"Where do you think you're going? Put those bags down and come give me a proper hello."

He dutifully did as she asked. They dropped their bags and embraced slowly. He had missed the physical contact, the warmth of feeling every time he was close to her. He rested his head on her shoulder and allowed himself to relax. Tension fell from him and he pulled her closer.

"It's good to be back."

"Don't you go anywhere again, ok?" She looked at him plaintively. He hated saying what he said next.

"Actually, we need to talk about that."

"But you just got back." She pushed away from him.

"Listen, I've done a lot of thinking. Let's go sit down because this is going to take a while."

They went to the living room and sat on the couch facing each other. He told her about simplifying his life by not aspiring to anything and how he was originally just going to give up promotions. Carefully he explained why he knew that he needed to buy his parents' house and move back and find a new job. The stuff about trying to move past the pain his parents caused he left out. He hated talking about that with her. He always felt so weak and unprotected after.

"Josh, this is a lot of stuff to process."

"I know. We don't have to talk about it all now."

"My life is here, Josh. I don't want to move. I can't."

He hated hearing this, but he wasn't surprised. He knew that there was a growing distance between them and that she didn't really like or understand all of this. Part of him felt that it would be better to start fresh. The rest of him was terrified of starting alone.

Looking downward he said, "I know, sweetie. I don't expect you to. I wish that you would, but I would never ask that of you."

"That's it?" she yelled indignantly. "All this time and you're just going to move away and say 'oh well'?" She turned from him and stared at the floor.

"You don't want to move. What am I supposed to do?"

"Have you even considered my feelings in any of this? Did you think of me at all?"

Sullenly, he answered, "No."

"I'm a part of your life, you know."

In a barely audible voice he said, "You were." He knew it was over between them. This was irreparable.

"What did you say? I *was*? What is wrong with you? Why are you so damn callous?"

He paused. Callous? He wasn't callous. He was straight forward. He was determined. He had a goal. He was all the things he was supposed to be. He was…ambitious. Ambitious. He sighed and shook his head. That was just what he was trying to escape. With good reason too, he supposed. It was making him miserable now.

"I have to do this. I know it's the right thing for me. I have to…"

Hurting her was not what he wanted to do, but on some level he knew it had been inevitable.

"I just can't believe you'd make a decision like this without talking to me. Quitting your job and leaving here and no discussion. Just random phone calls. And you wouldn't even tell me what was going on when you called. It's not right of you to do this, Josh."

He sat quietly and took it. She continued.

"We've been together for awhile now. We live together. There's a responsibility that goes with that. You randomly deciding to go bike riding for two weeks was one thing. I thought you'd go and get it out of your system, come back, and be fine. Instead, this. You're just irresponsible. And juvenile. It's like you can't grow up and you just run away from everything."

"I'm sorry, Anna. I don't know what else to do. I can't do this anymore," he said with a hint of defeat in his voice. Whenever she yelled at him, he felt so young. He felt like a child with no discipline. That feeling began to overtake him. "I'm going for a walk."

"Always running away!" she yelled after him as the door shut.

He walked down the street through his neighborhood. Everyone was shut up in their houses, windows shut and air conditioning running. A deep urge compelled him to run, to escape. He wanted a quiet place to hide. Somewhere where he could be alone without fear of discovery. It always tormented him that he could never find that in the city. He walked to the end of a dead end street and sat on the curb.

That hadn't gone well. Guilt pervaded him. He hadn't wanted to hurt her, but he couldn't do this anymore. He couldn't live in this city and play these games and pretend that he still bought into everything. He had found his truth and his direction and he would not compromise this.

Anna walked down the street toward him. She sat on the curb next to him.

He spoke first. "I'm so sorry..." He struggled to maintain his composure. He was steadfast in his decision, but he felt beaten down. The energy required for this battle with Anna was rapidly draining him.

"Josh, this isn't easy for me. I love you. I love you enough to not stand in your way. I don't want you to go away and I wish I could go with you. But just like you won't give up what you want your life to be, I won't give up what my life is here. Clearly, this wasn't meant to be."

They looked at each other closely. His eyes moved over the details of her face. He looked at her eyes, the curve of her eyelashes, the arch of her eyebrows, the angles of her nose, the way the lines of her lips ran together and pursed in the middle, the rounded delicacy of her chin. She was beautiful. She had been to him.

"I will miss you."

He stood and extended a hand to her. She took it and pulled herself up. They walked back in silence. He unpacked and prepared dinner. Exhausted, he went to bed after he finished. He took the couch and left her the bed.

Chapter 10

In the morning he ate breakfast and prepared himself to call his parents. He made sure to call early.

"Hello?"

"Hi, dad. How are you?"

"Fine. How are you? How's your ride going?"

"I'm good. I'm actually back from my ride. I'm in Rossdale."

"Couldn't do it, huh? I told you you weren't cut out for it."

"No, it wasn't that at all. Mom told me you guys were moving."

"You came back because of that? Why?"

"I want to buy the house."

"Why do you want to do that? You never come home now."

"I just don't have time to go home. But I like the house. I can't let you sell it to strangers." He lied without qualms. He wasn't about to tell his dad why he really couldn't go home. He refused to tell him how close it would come to destroying him each time and how his disgust for them grew. How he would come up with any excuse necessary not to go back. Briefly he worried that all these feelings would follow him to that house and that he would fail to beat the lingering memories.

"We would probably get more money if we put it on the market."

"But you'll save money on realtor fees. I'm not asking for a deal. I'll pay a fair price."

"I don't know. It goes up tomorrow. Your mother and I want to see what we can get for it. You can make an offer just like everyone else."

He was becoming annoyed now. "Dad, why won't you let me just buy the house? The house could be on the market for months. If you let me buy it now you don't have to wait or worry about it and you can go sit on a beach in Florida and drink martinis that much sooner."

"I'll talk it over with your mother and get back to you in a few days."

"Dad, you're putting in on the market tomorrow. Can't you give me an answer today?"

"We'll see."

"I'll call you in a few hours then."

"Fine, bye."

"Bye."

He never understood why his parents had to be so difficult. It was often like dealing with overgrown children. That was how he thought of them, especially since he used to have to take care of them. He refused to let himself relive it and cut short his train of thought.

He puttered around the apartment for a

few hours, cleaning and picking up and going through the week's worth of mail. Finally, he got tired of waiting and called.

"Hey dad."

"We haven't decided yet, Josh."

"Honestly, what is there to decide about? Do you not want me to have the house?"

"That's not it at all. We just want a fair price for it."

"I told you I'd give you a fair price. What's the problem?"

"We'll call you when we decide. Bye."

"Bye."

He didn't understand. He thought that they would be happy to sell it to him. Instead they had to give him the run around. They could never let anything be simple. He was convinced that they were taking pleasure in this.

Glumly, he finished washing dishes and started to fix his lunch for work the next day. He was looking forward to going in, but only because he'd be quitting. It occurred to him that he may have to wait a few days because he wanted to sort things out about the house first. This killed whatever excitement he had for work. He would have to suffer through the next few days. His parents had a way of ruining anything they were even remotely involved in.

As he stood cooking his chicken, he

remembered that he in fact had another week before he was expected back. He would have tomorrow free. He knew what to do.

He lay in bed that night trying to keep his resolve firm. The fact that this was much more difficult than he expected worried him. Was this a sign that he wasn't doing the right thing?

He stared up at the ceiling and listened to the house creak around him under the force of the wind. A strong wind always seemed more ominous to him than rain or snow. It could move things and knock them over and even kill. And yet it was invisible. It was an omnipresent power that was hidden from everyone, but whose effects could easily be seen. It intrigued him, but also scared him to an extent. It was an unknown. Listening to it force the trees to dance and the house to sway, he felt exposed. He pulled the blankets closer around him, searching for security, and willed himself to sleep.

As soon as he awoke the next morning he jumped out of bed. He threw on clothes, skipped showering and eating, and ran to the train. It would take him half way to his parents' house. Buses and taxis would cover the rest of the distance.

When he got close to town he gave the cabbie his parents' address, but instructed him to drive by and not stop. When they did this Josh took note of the realtor's name and phone number displayed in front of the house. He asked the driver to take him there. At the real estate office he located the realtor in charge of his parents' house. He introduced himself and made an offer for the exact amount his parents wanted.

The realtor was thrilled.

"I'm so impressed! The house just went on the market this morning. You must have been eyeing it for a while."

"Not too long, but I really wanted it."

"Well, it's yours unless they turn down the offer. Let me just give them a call and finalize things."

She went into her office and made a call. He watched her smile and nod at the air. She hung up and walked back.

"They were thrilled. They were surprised that anyone made an offer yet. They accepted."

"Excellent. That's great."

"I have to draw up the papers. Can you come back this afternoon to sign everything?"

"Sure, that sounds good."

He was satisfied. He walked out and hailed a taxi and gave his parents' address. With a smile he noted that soon it would be his address. He walked around to the back and in the back door. His mom was in the kitchen.

"Josh! You'll never guess what happened. We sold the house!"

"That's great, mom. That was quick."

"We even got exactly what we asked for. We're so happy. I hope whoever it is can finalize things soon so we can get out of here."

"Mom, why wouldn't you just sell the house to me?"

"We wanted to make sure we got the most for it as we could. We wouldn't feel right making you pay that much."

"But I offered to pay that much. I want you to get what it's worth too. And you wouldn't have had to pay commission."

"Well, there's no point in arguing now. It's been sold."

"You're right, it has. And I look forward to moving in."

"What?" Confusion washed over her face. He watched the understanding replace it, then anger. "You bought the house?" she demanded to know.

"Yes, mom. You wouldn't just sell it to me so I took dad's advice and just made a bid like anyone else could."

"Why would you do that?"

"What does it matter, mom? You get your money. You should be happy. What's wrong with me being happy?"

"Nothing, nothing at all. I'm glad you're happy. But now we've wasted all that money on the realtor. It seems silly."

He could no longer contain himself. "Mom, I told you this! I offered you a chance not to. You refused! Christ. Why do you do this?"

He refused to be in the same room with her any longer. He walked out into the yard and stood watching the sky. It was a clear day, with only a few sparse puffs of clouds littering the sky. He loved this spot and wished for it to be completely his.

Back in the kitchen, he said good-bye to his mother. Deciding that he still had some time to kill, he walked back to the realtor's office. When he got there she had finished preparing most of the documents.

"This will probably not get finished today. So I'll have you sign some of these and then tomorrow I will have the homeowners come in so we can finish the rest of it."

"Sure, that's fine. They've agreed to come in tomorrow?"

"Yes, I just got off the phone with them and they want to get everything squared away as soon as possible."

An hour later he called it a day. All the technical terms and legal phrasings had exhausted him. He didn't want to go all the way back to the city today. He debated between staying at the house for the night or getting a room somewhere. Deciding that it wasn't worth the money for a motel, he headed back to the house.

As he had hoped, his parents weren't up. Relief washed over him as he made his way up the stairs to his old bedroom. His parents had never bothered to do anything with it, though they kept saying they were going to convert it into a guest room. Childhood toys and trinkets still lined the shelves and were stored away under the bed and in the closets. Memories began to flood back but he steadfastly forced them down. He refused to deal with any of that now. He just wanted to sleep.

Slowly moving light and shadow on his eyelids woke him. The windows had never had curtains. At one point he had learned to sleep through it, but he had lost that skill and was grateful for that. He had a lot to do today and there was no point in wasting time sleeping.

He walked downstairs and into the kitchen. Both his parents were sitting, reading the paper, and drinking coffee. They turned in surprise as they heard him enter.

"We didn't realize you were here."

"Yeah, there was no point in going back to the city last night. There's still paperwork to sign today."

His mother glared at him for a second. "Indeed there is."

He made coffee and walked into the backyard. Shortly this would be his. The grass and the trees and the garden would belong to him. He'd have to learn to mow the lawn and trim the trees and weed and plant the garden. It would become his space and his retreat.

The door creaked open and he turned.

"Are you leaving now?"

"Yes."

"Were you going to tell me?"

"We figured you'd head over when you were ready."

"I'll catch a ride with you guys."

Always so juvenile. Couldn't they be mature and at least pretend to be civil? They were treating him as if he had stolen the house from them.

The next half hour was spent in silence. They only break from it was the realtor occasionally saying "Here" or "Initial this."

They parted ways without a word. There was still time before the end of the business day so he went to the bank to move forward with his mortgage. He wasn't too concerned about it going through, as he had good credit and some savings. He refrained from mentioning that he'd be quitting his job soon. Shortly before close he completed the application. He had some more paperwork to submit in the next few weeks. Then, he would be able to finalize moving and sending his parents packing. In the meantime, he would take care of getting the house inspected and appraised. As much as he'd like to trust his parents, he didn't and planned to document everything.

Deciding he was done with everything there, he called for a cab and began his trek back to the city.

When he got back Anna was waiting for him.

"Listen, I know we're not together, but you can't just take off and not tell me. I was worried about you. Where were you?"

"I bought the house. I had stuff to take care of."

Sadness crept into her eyes, but she didn't betray it in her voice. "So you're definitely going then?"

"Unless the mortgage doesn't go through for some reason, yes."

"Ok." She walked away.

He stood there expecting a fight or at least a discussion but she didn't come back. He heard the bedroom door close. The couch was his again. Hurting her was never his intention, but he kept making it worse. It would be good for both of them when he finally left. Living with her now was tortuous. They would ignore each other for hours on end. Sometimes he would catch her watching him with a mix of longing and sadness on her face. He would pretend not to see her as the waves of guilt washed over him. They needed the separation to be more than words or actions. It had to be space as well.

Chapter 11

Vacation ended and he went back to work. He didn't quit because he still didn't know if the house was actually his. As time passed he found it harder and harder to not participate in it all. All his coworkers were still fighting for success. It was hard to keep his competitive drive in check and not join in. The urge to get ahead was surging back in with a vengeance. He started to go back to his old routine, started to get himself and his work noticed again.

At home he found it harder to be around Anna but not be with her. She was keeping the apartment when he left, so until he got the house they were stuck together. She was still beautiful to him and he would crave her closeness. He began to want her back and didn't know what to do. They hadn't really ended the relationship. It was just decided that if he were leaving then they wouldn't continue it. He rationalized to himself that he hadn't left yet so there was no reason not to still be together. They became more affectionate each day. She allowed him to share the bed with her again.

By the time he got the call from the bank he didn't want to leave as much. His mortgage was approved. There was nothing to stop him from moving. He knew that he should. He had fought for this, but he had forgotten his reasons. Everyday life had swept him back up.

He forced himself to start preparing, though he was reluctant. As he packed he came across his bag from the trip that had never been cleaned out after he got back. He tossed the filthy clothes into a pile and sorted out his notebook, pens, camera, and leftover food. Not feeling motivated to pack, he went to get his film developed. The notebook came with him as well so he'd have something to do while he waited.

He dropped the film off and was told to come back in an hour. He sat on a bench outside and flipped through his notes. As he read what he wrote about Adelaide, he began to remember his reasons. It surprised him how easily he had been blinded by everyday life and drawn back into the routine. He was more determined now than ever to escape from this.

An hour had passed so went back to pick up his pictures. He flipped through them and paused at the one of the beach. If for no other reason, he wanted to move to be near the beach again. He hoped to someday be able to return to that beach, the site of his insight, and furthermore, his inspiration. When he did he hoped he would be able to be proud of where he was in life.

Anna hadn't heard his news about the mortgage so he headed home to tell her.

Already he was feeling guilty and ashamed, knowing he had led her on. He had known it couldn't go anywhere. He had known he would still move. And yet he had given in to immediate gratification with no thought as to the consequences. He had to escape this life. It was doing him no good and he was hurting others.

She was sitting on the couch reading a book.

"Hey, Anna. Reading anything good?"

"Just a girlie book. Nothing that you'd like."

"So, I got a call from the bank today."

He had her complete attention now. "And?"

"Everything is approved," he said quietly.

"Oh." She looked down. "Well, that's great. I'm really happy for you."

She looked back up and met his eyes. The unmitigated sadness there made him want to change his mind and stay, but he thought of Adelaide.

"I'm really sorry. You can still come with me if you want."

"You know I can't."

"I understand. I'll be leaving soon. I already started packing. I still have to call my parents and find out when they're leaving, though."

This exchange drained him. Doubt crept

back in. What if he was wrong about this? What if he were no happier than before? He would have no friends and no job and no girlfriend there. If he failed no one would care and no one would help him out.

The next morning he called his parents from work and found out that they would be leaving in two days. He was caught off guard by this. He had expected to have more time. There was no deadline to move, but if he didn't do it soon he knew his motivation would wane and he might forget his reasons again. So he packed up his personal belongings from his office and put things in order as best he could. He went to his manager, quit, and walked out while his boss was still searching for words.

The train ride home was packed and no one would let him sit. He struggled to not fall over and to keep his box of stuff from being knocked from his hands. Having space again would be such a relief.

It was the night before he was to leave. He sat down with Anna.

"Remember when I used to talk about truth?"

"That was awhile ago, but yes, vaguely."

"I couldn't understand it at all and how we all could get along."

"Yeah…"

"I've decided that we have our own personal truths. We find them and we live them and we get along with people because our truths intersect. Once we know these truths we are beholden to them. We're driven. That's where I'm coming from now. I know it's what I have to do. So I'm going to do it."

"I know. I know that I can't try to convince you to stay just like you can't convince me to leave. I still don't like it."

"I sort of think of it like our truths intersected for awhile, but it's time for them to diverge now."

"I guess."

Neither of them said anything else. They both stared at the floor, caught up in their own thoughts. Anna finally got up and walked out of the room. He heard the bedroom door close. He was shut out for the last time. This would be his last night here.

In the morning he loaded boxes into his rental van while Anna slept. She was still asleep when he was done. Not knowing what to say to her, he left his key on the kitchen table and walked out.

He pulled into the driveway of his parents' house, of his house. The completeness of his actions registered for the first time. All signs of them had been cleared from the yard. The windows were empty. There were no chairs on the back porch. Even the rope hanging from his favorite climbing tree was gone. He knew when he walked in that back door no one would be there. A sense of emptiness filled him and he felt desperately alone.

To distract himself he unloaded all his boxes and returned the van to the local drop off. He had left his bike in the van to ride home, thinking that the exertion would help burn off his concerns. Instead, the lack of pedestrians and cars that he was accustomed to left him nothing to focus on. He was left to his thoughts. Miserable, he couldn't bring himself to unpack. He dug out his sleeping bag and slept in the middle of the living room floor that night.

He was sore and stiff the next morning. He wandered into the kitchen to make breakfast. There was no food. There were no pots and pans. There wasn't even a refrigerator. He felt dumb. Normally he planned everything in exacting detail, yet somehow he had neglected to do so for the biggest thing in his life. The sheer amount of stuff he knew he needed to acquire overwhelmed him. He had no job and a mortgage and knew his savings would be used up quickly buying things for the house. He sighed. Not a good start at all. He rode his bike downtown to the grocery store and bought doughnuts, o.j., and a newspaper.

The remainder of the day he spent scouring the classifieds. He made a list of jobs to follow up on, found a cheap used fridge, lawnmower, and microwave. He decided things like a bed and bureau could wait until he was a bit more settled.

He rode around to restaurants the next morning inquiring about dishwasher positions. He had decided that dish washing was good, wholesome manual labor. There wasn't much in the way of advancement to distract him. No one would even pay much attention to him. It was perfect. The first three restaurants weren't hiring anymore. The fourth was, but he could tell that they were more interested in hiring teenagers who would work for less. Finally, at the fifth place he visited, they hired him on the spot. They were desperate for help and asked if he could start right then. He saw no reason not to and donned an apron and started in.

That day he only had to work three hours, but by the end of it he was exhausted. His arms were dead weight and his neck and backed ached. On his way out the manger stopped him.

"Can you work tomorrow?"

"Yeah, sure. What time?"

"10. We'll have you fill out paperwork before your shift."

"Ok. Will I be able to get a meal during my shift?"

"Of course. Did you eat anything tonight?"

"No."

"Grab something before you leave. See you tomorrow."

He bothered the cook for a burger and sat on an overturned milk crate in a corner to eat. It would be good to get free meals.

At home he sat down and figured out how much he'd be making a month. Sixty hours a week seemed like a reasonable amount to work. He did the math and stared at the paper. After taxes there would be no way he could pay the mortgage, let alone buy food or pay for electricity and heat.

He lay down in his sleeping bag. He had his space, but he couldn't afford to live. And what was he going to do with all this space anyhow? Never before had he had this much space to himself. Never before had he acted with so little thought.

The next few weeks he worked as much as they'd let him. They were pleased that he was so dependable. He was happy that they let him work all the time. The free meals and extra income made him feel a bit better. By the time he had to pay the mortgage he had just enough to pay for it. But each subsequent month he had to take money from his savings.

Summer was drawing to a close. He was running out of money and would soon have a heating bill to pay. They didn't have anymore hours to give him at work. He started looking for another job. Thoughts of Adelaide filled his mind more and more and he cursed her. She may have been able to get by somehow, but he couldn't. The stress of living on the edge of poverty made him miserable. He didn't know what to do. With each passing day the thought of moving back to the city and begging for his job back seemed more and more appealing. His dream seemed so foolish and unrealistic now.

One day he was washing dishes and lost in his thoughts. It dawned on him how he could get the extra money he needed. Currently he was living out of only two rooms in the house. The rest was sitting unused. If he rented out the other half of the house he'd have no problems paying for his mortgage. When he went home that night he looked through the classifieds to determined a fair price.

He walked through the half he was going to rent. He made mental notes of what should be fixed up. With any luck he'd be able to do most things himself and he could save some money.

He had a purpose again. Having a goal made him feel alive. Each morning and every night he would work on something. He spackled the holes in the walls and sanded it down. Once all the cosmetic blemishes of the walls were corrected he painted them. The bathroom proved to be the biggest task. He ripped up the rotting tiles, sanded the original floor and meticulously retiled. The aging medicine cabinet was replaced and the slanting ceiling repaired. The tub needed replacing, but he didn't feel comfortable doing that himself. His funds were running low, so he let it go.

Reasonably satisfied with the results, he called it done. He placed an ad and waited.

Calls began to trickle in. He saw one or two people every few days. He didn't rush the process. The kitchen and one bathroom would be shared so he needed to find someone he could get along with. Families with children, an elderly couple, three college students, and a middle-aged woman came to look. Some had dogs, some had birds, and one had five cats. Two weeks into his search a young couple came to look at it. They reminded him a bit of him and Anna. The man was slightly taller than himself with the same brown hair and wiry build. She had Anna's eyes. He forced himself not to watch her too much, for fear of scaring them off.

"So why are you renting it out?" the man inquired.

"It was my parents' house. With them gone it's much too big for just myself. There's no sense in letting the space go to waste."

He stood back in the hall as they looked around a room and quietly conferred in a corner.

The man came back. "My wife and I are definitely interested in renting it."

"Great. I have two more people to show the place to and I'll get back to you as soon as possible."

"Ok. Thanks very much."

He showed them to the door. He had

made up his mind already, but wanted to meet with the other two people to be sure. He was intrigued by this couple. It could have been Anna and him, if she had come with him. He felt a pang of remorse, but forced himself to think of Adelaide. He looked at the photo of the beach that he'd had blown up and framed. This had to have been the right decision.

He called the man back in a few days and told him that the place was his if he wanted it.

They moved in a week and a half later. They had few possessions, but enough to fill their half of the house. It was more than he had. He felt unburdened as they moved their belongings in. He would be able to get by now. And he could watch what his life could have been play out.

In a way, they made him feel juvenile. They were following the prescribed societal path and he was goofing off. He was single, without a real job, and with no prospects. He felt belittled, but refused to give up yet. He was determined that this would pay off.

Chapter 12

Chris and Julia helped to keep him grounded. In the evenings he would chat with them as they all cooked dinner. Some nights he would bring them home something from the restaurant. Julia was helping him learn to cook. He had never lived on his own before and only knew the basics. Anna had always cooked for him before. Before that was mostly takeout and frozen meals.

With the extra income he was able to cut back his hours a bit. With the extra time he began to paint and draw again. He had moved far from his art over the past few years. It wasn't intentional, he simply had been too busy and caught up in life.

In the evenings he would go into his backyard and paint the trees and other plants. As darkness fell he would move inside and sketch objects around the house. As it grew increasingly colder he did more and more of his work inside. Soon he had all but exhausted the interesting objects in the house. He began to add abstract elements to his work to bring new life to it. He was pleased with all the work he was producing.

Even as the temperature dropped he still rode his bike to work. He kept meaning to get a car, but didn't feel inclined to spend the money or go through the hassle. It made him happy to pedal around town. The roads were quieter here so he could enjoy the ride instead of challenging the cars and pedestrians as he had done in the city.

The holiday season began to draw near. In the past he had begrudgingly spent it with his parents, but he had no intention of flying to Florida this year.

"Josh, what are you doing for Thanksgiving?" Julia asked.

"Nothing much. Just staying here."

"By yourself? What about your parents?"

"They're in Florida. I don't mind spending the day by myself. It's not really an important holiday."

"Well, if you're not doing anything you're more than welcome to join Chris and me."

"Thanks, I appreciate the offer. I'll probably do that. I can help you cook too, if you want."

In addition to working on his art more, he had also been devoting copious amounts of time to cooking. His skills had improved tenfold and he was now quite handy in the kitchen. It was mostly due to Julia's patience and time with him. He always enjoyed the time he spent with her, but her eyes were a constant reminder of Anna and haunted him.

He had spoken to Anna only once since he left. Since then, he hadn't let himself. He reminded himself that they needed space from each other and refused to intrude upon her's any more. At work he had too much time to think of her and had started to dislike the amount of time he had with his thoughts there.

He had been at his job for six months. They were extremely pleased with him. He was never late and diligently did his work every shift. They tried to promote him to busboy, but he declined. It wouldn't be acceptable to get promoted. He didn't want to advance. Part of him was confused though because he knew that he hadn't tried to get the promotion.

That was really the only thing he was trying to escape, that constant fight for advancement. But this had been offered to him without a fight. He was unsure if that meant he should accept. It would be extra income, which was always useful. As he had this internal debate, he also wondered if he had indeed in some way been trying to get promoted. Perhaps he had been working too hard. Perhaps he had made himself too noticeable. He considered backing off a bit and maybe being late a day or two and taking a slightly long break. He never followed through on this because he did not want to disappoint his manager and coworkers.

On Thanksgiving he helped prepare the

meal. He made mashed potatoes and stuffing and carrots. He tried to make gravy, but it was substantially more difficult than he anticipated. It was a thick and pale mass before he conceded defeat and turned it over to Julia's superior skills. She told him that everything would be done at two and suggested he go change. He went upstairs and selected khakis, a button down shirt, and a tie from his closet. His undershirts and socks sat in piles on the floor. He had never bothered to get a bureau. It had only been a few weeks ago that he had purchased a mattress. He still didn't have a bed frame for it, or sheets, so he slept on top of it in his sleeping bag.

He got dressed and went back downstairs. It was a little before two and a woman was standing in the kitchen. Julia introduced her.

"Josh, this is Mary. She's a teacher at the high school. I had been telling her about you and she wanted to meet you."

"Uh, hi. It's nice to meet you." He was being set up. He was confused. The woman seemed nice enough, but did he even want to get to know any women? He wasn't sure that he did. He couldn't remember how dating had fit into the plan.

He conversed pleasantly throughout the meal. After, Chris and Julia excused themselves and left him alone with Mary.

"So what do you teach at the high

school?"

"Ninth grade English. I've been teaching for five years now."

"Do you like it?"

"Some days more than others. They can be a difficult age group to work with. Aside from just trying to keep them interested in the material, there's always some thing or another going on that's more interesting. Two friends fighting, an unlikely couple… Those are much more interesting than Shakespeare."

"Is it rewarding, though?"

"Yes. Every now and then I can see that I'm getting through to them, that someone's taking more than a cursory interest. That's what makes it worth it."

They chatted for several hours. He refused to let himself open up too much with her because he still hadn't decided whether dating fit into his plan. Finally, she said that she should be going and they made plans to meet for coffee in a couple days. He planned to figure out before then if he could indeed date.

The next morning Julia inquired as to how things had gone. He told her what had transpired and thanked her for inviting Mary.

At work that day he busied himself with thinking about where dating fit into his plan. He reasoned that his goal was to be happy and he wanted to do that by not wanting things. By extension, he should not want to date either. But there was the chance that being with someone could make him happier. To date without any expectations would be next to impossible, though. To continue seeing Mary would be ok because he hadn't gone out in search of her, she had been introduced to him. But if they continued dating there would inevitably be expectations. He wondered whether Adelaide had a boyfriend. This was all more difficult than he expected. Finally, he decided that he would continue to see Mary, if she wanted to see him, and he just wouldn't push anything. He would evaluate where things were and if he started to have expectations, that would be the end of it.

They met for coffee and several more times after that. She, like Anna, was intrigued with his view of things. For some reason, knowing that he had chosen to be a lowly dishwasher and had voluntarily given up a well-paying job made him appealing to her.

She would have happily continued to see him, but Josh wasn't as happy. He became dissatisfied with the routine they fell into. It was expected that they would go out either Friday or Saturday night, depending on when he was working. It was expected that they would talk every day. While he didn't mind any of these things, he worried that he was reverting back to old habits. Remembering how Anna had taken this and all that had transpired after, he was wary of explaining himself to Mary. He opted to simply distance himself from her slowly and let things take their course.

Something kept bothering him. While he was sorting through all these things in his head, the concept of expectations kept troubling him. He thought he would be happier without aspirations or expectations. But he began to realize that there was a whole new set of expectations in this life. The restaurant expected him to show up. He expected Chris and Julia to pay rent each month. Where he was to draw the line he didn't know. So he simply affirmed his commitment to not aspire to anything and comforted himself with that.

Chapter 13

Things with Mary finally ended. She voiced her dissatisfaction with how little they were seeing and talking to each other and ended it. He was overly relieved to not have to be doing the breaking up this time. Julia knew that it was his fault, though.

"I thought you liked her," she said one night while they worked on dinner.

"I did. But things change."

"What changed?"

"I'm just not at a place in my life where I want to be dating."

"So you decided to lead her on?"

"No, that wasn't it at all. I didn't know how things would go when we first started talking. I wanted to give it a chance. It just didn't work out."

"I guess I won't be helping you out again."

"I didn't ask for help."

"I know. You just seemed lonely."

"I'm not. I like being by myself," he insisted, defensively.

"That's fine. I won't try to help again."

This exchange upset him. He did not want to anger Julia, but he didn't need her taking pity on him. He wondered if he had violated some unwritten landlord/tenant rule by becoming friendly with Chris and her. Her similarities to Anna had emboldened him and he knew that he had become friendly with her more quickly than he would have with someone else. He had trouble keeping his thoughts and feelings toward Anna separate from his ones about Julia.

The shared time in the kitchen became painfully silent. The couple gave their 30 day notice a few weeks later and moved out at the end of the next month.

Having grown accustomed to the extra income and the fewer hours it required him to work, he searched again for a new tenant. This time he wasn't as concerned about finding someone he could get along with. He planned on spending less time with whoever moved in this time, preferably none at all.

"So you work in the city?"

"Yeah. The commute's a bitch, but it's worth having the extra space here."

The man was in his mid-30s and said he worked at a marketing company in Rossdale. Josh felt that he would be a good tenant and planned to offer the apartment to him.

"The space is nice. I used to work in the city too, but I got tired of it. I moved here because this way my parents' house and they moved to Florida. I wasn't really up to the commute though. I just got a job here."

"What do you do?"

"I used to be an artist at a design firm, but now I'm a dishwasher."

"Are you serious? What, no design jobs around here?"

"I didn't even look. I got tired of the rat race."

"Huh. Damn."

"I like it better. Less stressful." Josh wasn't sure if it was, but he did think it seemed better than before.

They talked some more and Josh offered him the room. Nick accepted and moved in shortly.

After a few months of living with Nick it occurred to him why he was curious about Nick and why he chose to live with him. Nick was who he would have been--relatively successful, working at a good firm in the city. Moving to the suburbs because he could afford the space and the commute. He began to watch him with an intense interest. Was he happy? That was all he wanted to know. On some level he desperately wanted Nick to be miserable. Otherwise, how could he know if all of this had been worth it? He needed to know that this was worth the sacrifice.

Though he didn't see Nick often, he suspected that he was indeed satisfied with his life. Occasionally he would bring work home and sit at the kitchen table writing and drinking coffee. At these times that dead glaze would permeate his eyes. But it was only those times. Josh wondered about his. He didn't know how to reconcile this disparate information. He though it was all or nothing. Nick was showing him this wasn't the case. Losing one's self at work didn't mean that one was lost everywhere, apparently. This gave him pause.

Adelaide had been happy at work, though, so he knew that was possible. He knew that he wasn't as happy as she was at work. He was happier than he had been before. There was so much less stress. All he had to do was show up and not break anything.

Outside of work he was relatively content. He figured that not having the stress of work carrying over made it better overall. There was a nagging boredom creeping up on him. He picked up some more hours at work to fill some time.

He also took up reading again. He told himself that it was just to have something to do, but somewhere in his head he knew that he was searching for the truth again.

One weekend he decided to go for a long ride again. He had only been riding around town and wanted to get away. He rode for a while and realized he was drawing closer to the city. This realization triggered a desperate desire to see Anna again. He rode to his old apartment, wondering if she'd still be living there. He stopped a little ways down and watched the house. The curtains still looked the same, the familiar peach color he always disliked. He walked his bike over to the stairs, lifted it to his shoulder, and walked up. He hesitated, then pressed the buzzer. A male voice answered.

"Hello?"

"Hi. I'm looking for Anna."

"Who's this?"

"An old friend of hers, Josh."

There was no response. Then he heard the door being unlocked.

"Josh who used to live here?"

"Yeah."

"What the hell do you want?"

The hostility surprised him. "I just wanted to say hi, that's all."

"She doesn't want to see you, you bastard."

He heard her call down the hall. "Who is it?"

"That guy Josh."

She peaked her head under the guy's arm, which was blocking the door.

"Josh."

"Hi Anna. I was out for a ride and was over here and—"

She made a motion for him to be quiet. "Let's go for a walk."

She turned to the man, said something to him quietly and he sullenly went back into the apartment.

The door closed and she walked

towards him. "You should have called."

"I'm sorry. I didn't realize…" He didn't know what else to say and let the thought trail off.

He continued without thought. "I'm sorry for how things ended."

"You didn't even say good-bye," she said accusatorily. The pain and anger were overwhelmingly clear in her eyes.

"You were asleep."

"Asleep? The last time I would have seen you and you think you couldn't wake me up? Instead I wake up to find your key on the table and you gone! And then nothing. One call and then no contact until now. Do you know how much that hurt?" She quickened her pace and he jogged a few paces to keep up.

"I'm sorry," was all he said, barely audibly. "I never meant to hurt you. I didn't stop loving you. But I had to do what was best for me. It didn't make it any easier on me."

"And you suppose it was easy on me? I didn't want it. It was your fault. Did it at least make you happy?"

He looked down and did not answer. She kept staring at him, waiting. He wasn't sure if he was happy. He didn't know anymore. "I don't know."

She shook her head. "You threw us away, cut off communication, and you don't know. What was the point?"

"I had to try. I didn't want to end up

dead inside. I at least accomplished that."

"Well, you killed a substantial piece of me. I'm glad you could spare a piece of yourself." She was becoming more and more spiteful. He realized he shouldn't have come. He was stirring up memories that were better left at rest.

They walked in silence and he looked up, taking notice of the contrast between the rooftops and the sky. There was a beautiful simplicity in the line they etched into the skyline.

"So who's the guy?"

"My boyfriend. He was my rebound after you left and he stuck. We're getting married next year."

He was surprised to hear this. They had discussed marriage, but she was opposed at the time. This guy must be better for her. That knowledge cut him deep. He always harbored a notion that what they had was special and could not be replaced or superseded. Despite the fact that he had chosen to end it, knowing she had moved on and replaced him filled him with an oppressive pain. He wished briefly to take it all back. Just as quickly he forced himself to think of Adelaide.

They parted ways and he rode slowly home. He went up to his room and sat on the bed and looked out over the back yard. The sun was nearly set and a few wisps of pink cut through the tree line. He looked above the treetops and saw the first few stars starting to appear. He wished to escape. That familiar urge to run overtook him.

Reason took hold and he went to his bike and rode to the beach. He left his shoes and socks in a pile by the bike.

The sand covered his toes, then the ocean washed it off. The cold numbed his toes. He did not retreat, but instead waded deeper. The water soaked up his pants and numbed his calves. A few more steps and his pants were drenched and everything up to his waist began to lose feeling. A wave came and soaked him up to his shoulders. He walked further. The water was up to his chin. He held his breath and went under. The cold ripped through his head in a blinding flash. He felt a horrid throbbing and started feeling distanced from his body. He pushed off the bottom and thrashed his head above the water. Crying now, he went under again. He stayed below until he began to lose himself. Back up he went.

The air felt warm against his skin. Defeated, he moved back toward shore. He could numb his body, but the pain was untouched. Into the sand he fell. He curled up into himself and sobbed.

The tears finally exhausted him and he rolled on his back and looked to the sky. Peace washed over him, but it was not one of happiness. It was the calmness of thorough, deadening defeat. Knowing he could do no more, he struggled to his feet. He rode home with sand filling his shoes and gusting behind him. Once home he did not wash. He lie down on the floor and fitfully fell asleep.

He awoke early, stiff and cold. The sand and salt had crusted over him and made his face ache as he yawned. He stumbled to the bathroom and took a cold shower. That morning he sat in his backyard and stared at the grass and the trees for hours. He knew he was lost again.

At work that afternoon, he focused on the dishes. He willed his mind blank and ignored the outside world. After several hours someone shook his shoulder and told him his shift was over. He clocked out and rode home. There were few cars on the road, but he noticed none.

Once home, he sat in the kitchen and slowly ate dinner. Nick came in and greeted him but his words did not register. He went to his room and read until he fell asleep, many hours later.

Chapter 14

The next day he awoke before dawn and rode to the seawall. On the way he picked up o.j. and a doughnut. He breathed in the salty air and watched the sun ascend. When he finished eating he removed his sketchpad from his bag and began to sketch the sea. As he drew the tiny details of the whitecaps and the ships barely visible again the horizon, calmness filled him.

He knew that it was just temporary, but it gave him hope. He made a point to draw every day. Why he had lost that habit he didn't know. Art had fallen into the background. He stopped reading and called art his answer. Sometimes he would create a painting from a sketch, filling in the colors by memory. These he would hang around the house. Nick always commented when he did and said he enjoyed them.

"Why don't you sell any of them? Or at least put them in a gallery?"

"Never felt like it."

"They're good. You should."

"They're nothing special. Anyone can paint the ocean. A million people have."

"Yours are different. There's something about them."

"Maybe I will someday."

Josh's paintings were different. They weren't the typical landscapes most created. There was an intriguing darkness to them. He painted his pain into them. Most painted their joy.

"Hey Josh, I want you to meet someone."

A well-dressed woman was looking around the kitchen.

"This is Emily. She's a friend from work. She's on the board at a small gallery a few towns over. I wanted her to see your work."

He did not want to talk to her, but was infallibly polite. "Hi Emily. It's very nice to meet you."

"Nick said you were a bit shy about your work, but he's been raving about it so I had to come take a look. I hope you don't mind."

"Oh, no, not at all. I'm glad you could come."

"You do have some lovely pieces. You say you've never showed them?"

"No, I've never tried to."

"That's a shame, you really should. I would love to show a few pieces at the gallery, if you don't mind."

"I don't know. I'll have to think about it."

"You should. It can't hurt. Maybe you could sell a few and fix this place up a bit."

He looked around. She was right, he should work on the house. He hadn't since he moved in and the years of neglect were showing.

"Do you have a card? I'll think about it and give you a call."

"Of course," she said and produced one from her purse.

They exchanged a few pleasantries and then he excused himself, leaving Emily and Nick standing in the kitchen.

Up in his room, he stood looking over the backyard. He debated whether or not to show his work. He didn't know if he wanted others to see it. The paintings he created were for himself. They were his release. They were how he expressed himself. How could anyone else understand what they meant? No one else would see them as he did. They would be trivialized. People would assign their own meaning to them.

The sun had sunk low enough that it was just touching the tree tops. They were golden, framed by brilliant pinks and blues.

Quietly, he spoke aloud. "No one sees the sunset the same way, but all get to experience it."

If people wanted to see his work, he would not stop it. They could assign their own meaning to it. He would always know the true one.

The next evening after work, he called

Emily. She had not expected to hear from him and was pleasantly surprised when he agreed to allow her to exhibit a few of his pictures. They spoke briefly and agreed to meet again the following week.

Each night he anguished over which to give her. Some were simply too personal and he was uncomfortable sharing those. Some he felt weren't deep enough and weren't a good example of his work.

He finally selected one of him thrashing in the night ocean, one of the neighborhood he used to live in, and one of Adelaide looking over the morning ocean. The one of Adelaide was the hardest to include because he was so close to it, but for the same reason he chose to show it. It was his most beautiful paining and he wanted to share that.

Emily came over and he showed her his choices and she approved. As he had hoped, she especially liked Adelaide.

"Who is the girl? A girlfriend?"

"No, a waitress I encountered one spring when I rode down the coast."

"Where were you driving to?"

"Nowhere special. I just wanted to go for a bike ride."

"Oh, you biked? That's really impressive."

"Thanks, it was fun." And it changed my life, he thought to himself.

They talked further and she told him

he'd need to come up with titles, dates, and brief descriptions for the works. She would come back in a few days for those and the pictures.

She stopped as he walked her to the door.

"What are you doing Wednesday night?"

"No plans."

"There's a reception at the gallery. You should come."

He hesitated. It had been years since he attended a social function. "If it's all the same to you, I think I'll pass."

"Are you sure? You'd get a chance to meet some other local artists. I'd really love it if you went."

"No, it's ok. It's not really my thing. Thanks for the invite though." He turned and opened the door for her, missing the disappointment flash across her face.

"It's at 9 if you change your mind. Good night."

"Good night." He closed the door and went to work on a new piece he had started.

When she came to collect the pieces she informed that there would be a reception for him and he was expected to be there. He refused, but she didn't back down. He finally agreed but had no intention of going.

The night of the reception she was waiting at his door when he got home from work.

"Hi."

"Hi. You need to get changed."

"Actually, I don't think I'm going to go."

"No, you are."

"I don't have a suit." She was wearing a form fitting long black dress. Nothing he owned would be appropriate.

"Yes, you do. It's in the kitchen. Go get dressed."

He stared at her for a moment. At a loss, he finally simply complied. There was a new gray suit hanging in the kitchen with a light blue shirt and black shoes. He was dumbfounded as to why she had done this and decided it would be best to simply do as she asked and not balk too much. He brought the clothes up to his room, showered, and got dressed.

She was waiting patiently in the kitchen when he came back down.

"The car's outside. Let's go."

"Ok."

He had never been to the gallery before. It was a beautiful structure. She led him inside to where his work was. A whole wall had been devoted to his three paintings. He liked the way they looked, well-lit and nicely framed.

"It looks good."

"I hoped you would like it."

"I thought you said this was a reception.

Where is everyone?"

"In the other room. Do you want to go in?"

He didn't want to, but knew he didn't have a choice. He mentally braced himself and agreed.

Chapter 15

As things progressed with Emily, he found all the same questions bubbling back up. Things with her were good, but he knew that she wasn't his answer. It had been years since he had moved out here, away from his city life, away from what he thought was holding him back. It had taken awhile, but he was finally starting to admit to himself that it hadn't fixed anything. It was a new life with a new set of problems. That wasn't to say he didn't like it better. He slept much better at night and it was great to be able to say he had a house.

Was happiness even an achievable goal? When he thought of finally finding it, doubt filled his head. It was beginning to seem like an impossible pipe dream.

Every morning now, barring downpours or subzero temperatures, he would ride down to the ocean. Summers used to be the only time he would ride down there, but he had come to appreciate watching the seasons pass and the ocean change from clear blue to a deep greenish-blue.

This time he used to really question himself. No longer was it a question of what he should do or what might make him happy. It was a question of who he was. Years of arbitrary rules had caused him to stop wondering this.

The more he questioned this, the more restless he grew. It was as if he had allowed himself to be dormant for years. And now he was feeling something in the pit of his stomach and he knew he couldn't make it rest anymore.

"Emily, what do you see in me?"

"I see a lot in you. You're handsome and talented and —"

"No, no. Not why do you date me. What kind of person do you think I am? What makes me me?"

"I don't know how well I can answer that. That's something you need to answer for yourself. But I do know that you won't take the status quo. And you have a lot of talent. And...well, quite honestly, you seem a little lost."

He hadn't talked to her about that at all. How obvious was it that he didn't know what to do with himself most of the time?

"So what would you say you're all about?"

"What, you haven't figured that out yet? What kind of boyfriend are you?" she teased. "I like art, I like sharing it with people. I just sort of fell into what I do now. I had wanted to be a sculptor. I went to art school and tried to make a living at it when I was done. But nothing ever sold and I realized that I wasn't very good at it and no one ever had the guts to tell me."

"I'm sure you were great."

She laughed. "Actually, no, I was terrible. A few years after I gave it up I dug up some of my pieces and they were horrible. I was embarrassed that I tried to get people to buy them.

"So I found myself with a fairly useless art degree and no idea what to do with myself. I ended up volunteering at a local gallery while I sorted through my options. And after a few months it dawned on me that I *liked* it. Even though I wasn't getting a paycheck, I looked forward to going to work. When a paid position opened up I applied and, well, here I am today."

"That's great that it worked out like that."

"I guess I am pretty lucky. Why do you ask, though?"

"C'mon, I'm a dishwasher. This isn't exactly my dream job."

"You seem pretty happy doing it."

He shrugged. "I like to tell myself I am."

"So what is it you'd like to do?"

"Damned if I know. I stopped wondering that years ago. I've been busy thinking that a job was just a source of money and nothing more so it didn't really matter. But I was wrong. Really wrong. There's got to be more to life than this."

"I wouldn't worry about it. You'll find

your answer."

He hoped so but didn't have too much faith. Everyone else seemed to fall into his or hers so easily. Had he screwed everything up too badly so far that he'd never find it now?

At a loss of what to do, he decided he would come full circle. Knowing that some of his skills were a bit rusty, he headed off to the library to find some books to review. As he haphazardly searched for the design books, he passed by the religion section. Remembering that Eastern religions had piqued his interest years ago in high school, he grabbed one off the shelf.

It took a few weeks, but he build his confidence up enough that he felt ready to get out there again. The classifieds yielded scant results, but it was a good enough start. He just hoped that someone would bother to call back after they saw his six-year stint as a dishwasher.

No one did. He kept applying and looked into getting a car so he could expand his search radius.

On his next trip to the library he was reminded about his overdue book. The Eastern religion book had fallen by the wayside during he job search. He made a point of picking it up when he got home so he could return it the next day. That evening he passed by it again and decided it would be a shame to return it unread.

To his surprise, as he read through it, he felt something. All the talk of being one with the world, of being at peace, of letting go of material and petty things stirred something in his belly. It was the feeling of the ocean, of the open road, of the cloudless night sky. The feeling he lusted after, tried desperately to find in his everyday life and it was in this book.

And in that instant he wanted to live life. He wanted to run to his backyard, stand on the hill, and yell to the woods. Or get on his bike and ride for hours. He wanted to go see the world. But instead he reclined back into the chair and stared at the ceiling. He had wasted so many years. So many. The stark realization of the futility of his life so far, the failure of his grand plan, all that he had given up, it made him want to resign himself to the failure his life would be.

In the morning he awoke, still in the chair staring at the ceiling, with the book splayed open beside him. Things felt different, but not in any sort of quantifiable way. He shrugged it off and set off on his morning bike ride. On his way back he stopped by the library to renew the book.

He wanted to keep reading it, but he had his first interview later that day. He had found his suit, which though slightly big, still looked presentable. It had been an awful ride home from the drycleaners, the bag catching the wind the whole way, but he and the suit had made it back intact.

He showered and shaved, checking for stray hairs along the side of his neck that he tended to miss and got dressed. It felt strange to be spending this much time on his appearance. At the risk of looking foolish, he tied his right pant let up to his knee to keep it out of the chain and set off.

The reception area was beautifully appointed. The elegant sterility caused him to pause just inside the entryway as memories from his days in the city came flooding back. This world seemed so bizarre and...inhospitable was the only word he could come up with.

"Can I help you?"

The receptionist looked at him expectantly.

Despite an array of misgivings, he introduced himself and gave his interviewer's name.

The interview was a strange thing.

"Where do you see yourself in five years?"

He didn't even know where he saw himself in five days or five months. Remembering some of the books he had read, he took a chance. "Doing your job."

The man laughed and gave him a friendly slap on the back. "That's what I like to hear, a good aggressive attitude.

"But I do have a question about your job

experience for the past couple of years."

Josh took a breath and began reciting the lie he had practiced. "I had a great job in the city, but then my dad got sick. My mom couldn't take care of him on her own, so I moved down here. The dishwashing job was flexible, so it worked. But my parents recently moved down to Florida to live in one of those assisted living communities, so I'm eager to get back into the game."

"Good man."

He didn't think the interview was tremendously successful, but he got a call back a couple days later. He knew they were taking a chance on him, so he felt obligated to take the job.

"Remember when I told you about what I used to do before I moved here?"

She looked at him curiously. "Yes, design work for an agency."

"I got a job doing that again."

"But you moved here to get away from that."

"I know. But getting away from that hasn't made me any happier. I feel like I should give it a chance again."

She was clearly disappointed in him. He was disappointed in him. But he couldn't say that it wouldn't be nice to have a steady paycheck, normal hours, and extra money.

A few weeks in he had settled into his groove. He got his first paycheck and took

Emily out to celebrate. She seemed perturbed throughout the meal. As they finished up their entrees--smoked salmon with light cream sauce for him and filet mignon for her--he finally asked her.

"Do you really want to know what's wrong?"

"Of course. Is the food bad? Are you not having a good time?"

"The food is fine. I'm just not thrilled about what we're celebrating. But I'm glad that you're happy."

He sincerely wished that she hadn't brought up happiness. Nothing he did made him happy. As soon as the novelty wore off he was back to being miserable. At least he had money now.

That night he sat down to make a list of things that made him happy. The ocean was undoubtedly first. The open night sky came next. Bike riding, painting, and reading. Emily. The smell of spring. Fresh fallen snow. Well, nature in general. He couldn't think of anything else. So, in fact, some things did make him happy. But where did that get him? He couldn't make a life around the smell of spring and the ocean.

The night was clear, though cool. The grass was damp and cold on his bare feet, but he lay down anyhow. As he gazed up into the sky, taking note of the little and big dipper, the only two constellations he could consistently recognize, he felt at peace. He wondered why this calmed him so. There was something in the back of his mind telling him if he could figure this out, he just might be satisfied with life.

Gradually this notion faded from the front of his mind. Work got busy and several hours of overtime became a weekly routine. It didn't take long before he had enough to buy a used car. After that, the bike sat unused more and more. Not accustomed to having extra money, he amused himself with the best of everything he could think of. The constant stream of purchases kept him well sated.

The Eastern religion book was returned a couple months late, but read no further than he had gotten that one night. It wasn't something he thought about now. Between work and his new possessions, he didn't have the time he used to.

Emily asked one day why he had stopped showing her his paintings.

Sheepishly, he muttered, "I haven't painted any."

"You've stopped painting?"

"Well, I've been busy with work. I haven't really had the chance. Besides, I haven't really felt inspired."

She said nothing more on the subject.

He had felt her growing increasingly distanced from him and knew this didn't help. She hadn't wanted him to take the job, though she never said it.

"You've changed, Josh."

"Why do you say that? Because I've got a job?"

"No, not because of-- No, you know what? Yes, because you've got a job. Ever since you got this job the things I loved in you when we first met have been fading away. It's like you've retreated off to some other world. You don't even paint anymore!"

"I'm sure I'll start painting again."

"But, Josh, is it even in you anymore? Because I feel like you've closed a part of yourself off."

He hated being challenged like this. "What do you want me to do, quit my job, go back to being a dishwasher? Look at all I can have now!" He gestured around his living room.

"Are you going to tell me that these things make you happy?"

"Yes," he said defiantly, "they do."

With a hint of sadness in her eyes, she stood up. "Josh, I do not want to be with this person you've become. It's not you."

The door closed behind her, but he didn't move from his chair. He loved her, but he didn't think it was fair of her to expect him to give up his newfound life.

Having no commitments now other than work, he began putting it longer hours. After not too long, this was recognized with a promotion. He took this as a sign that he was heading in the right direction.

There was a hint of loneliness tingeing his happiness. He had no one to share his news with other than Nick. There was no one to celebrate with.

And so he decided he'd buy himself something to celebrate. Something big.

His car, which had seemed perfectly adequate yesterday and gave him no problems, seemed a good candidate for an upgrade. He deserved something that reflected his success. That weekend he set off to the local dealerships to get an idea of what was out there. By the end of the day he had narrowed down his choices to a handful of sporty convertibles. He went home to sleep on it.

As he was driving home a car caught his eye. It was partially obscured by a low-hanging tree, but he saw enough to see a for sale sign and that it was a classic Ford Mustang convertible. This was a car that he had always hoped to own since he was a teenager.

He checked his rearview mirror, slammed on his brakes, and turned around in the middle of the road. Pulling onto the side of the road, he took a closer look at the car. It was royal blue, with a white top that was in rough shape. He noticed a good size dent in the driver's door. Undoubtedly, it needed a lot of work. He got out and walked to the front door of the house. No one answered so he committed the number on the sign to memory and drove back home. As soon as he got there he called and left a message.

Thinking about the car and fixing it up filled him with an urge to create. Despite the fact that he designed every day at work, this creative urge had fallen silent since he began working there. The strength of this desire surprised him.

The owner of the car didn't call back that week. By the time the weekend rolled around, the creative urge slumbered again and he had settled on a convertible to buy.

Saturday he got up early to head over to the dealership. He had heard stories of people spending the better part of the day haggling over the price and working out details and he wanted to be sure to have time to drive the car around before dark.

The phone rang just as he got out of the shower. He ran over to it and answered one ring ahead of the machine.

"Hello?"

"Hi, is this Josh?"

"Yes."

"This is Rick. I'm the guy with the Mustang convertible. I just got back from vacation yesterday so I couldn't call you sooner."

"That's ok. So what sort of shape is the car in?"

"Well, it runs. But it needs a lot of work.

I've been letting her sit in the backyard unused for a couple years now. It's a shame to do that to her. So I knew it was time to sell. She's a good project car."

"Could I come over and take a look at it a little later?"

"Sure thing. I'll be around unpacking for the next couple hours."

"Great, I'll be over in an hour."

He knew he was going to buy the car no matter what kind of shape it was in. Though he knew nothing about cars other than how to check his oil, he was confident that he could restore it.

After a harried trip to the bank to get enough cash before it closed, he dug out his bike and set off. Upon closer inspection of the car, it was obvious that it would need more than just a little work. Undeterred, he simply negotiated accordingly.

It took a good ten minutes to get the car going, but it did in fact run. He broke down his bike and put the frame in the back seat and the tires in the front. It was a slow ride. He drove 25 mph with his hazards on the whole way home.

At the library he located several books on basic car maintenance and ordered one specifically on older Mustangs. The rest of the weekend was spent making a list of tools to buy and things to look at first. He wanted to get the engine running well before he dug into getting the car looking as it should.

By Monday he had a decent idea of where to start with everything. For the first time in months he left work on time. The auto parts store near him closed at 6 and he didn't want to be rushed since he didn't really know what he was looking for. And he wasn't inclined to ask for help. He knew the salesperson would want to talk cars and he didn't feel like looking dumb.

At five of six he had found most of what was on his list. Several hundred dollars lighter, he ventured home, popped the hood of the Mustang, and lay the assorted tools out in front of it. He looked at the engine, looked at the tools, and realized that he might need to take a class.

Every day that week he left work on time. And the following week. He was gaining an understanding of how everything worked in theory, but he still wasn't comfortable working under the hood. The engine wasn't as easy to decipher as the labeled and color-coded diagram in his book.

As he prepared to leave work the next Monday, his boss stopped him.

"New lady in your life?"

"Huh? Oh, no. No lady actually. A car."

"Must be a pretty nice car to pry you away from here," he joked.

"No, not yet. I'm hoping it will be. It's an old Mustang that's pretty beat up."

"You'll have to take me for a ride once it's done. Just make sure things don't start sliding around here. You're on track to go far."

He bristled at this, but agreed and left.

He didn't know any of the hands-on details of cars. He started off simple—checking the fluids and changing the oil. The oil change turned into a messy several day project.

Knowing he was out of his league, he signed up for a continuing education class in auto repair. Becoming increasingly aware of his rapidly falling status at work, he went back to working late every night but Tuesday. Tuesday from six until nine he learned how to fix up his car.

The Mustang began running more smoothly. It made him happy to be working on it, watching it come together. It was immensely more satisfying to slowly build it up than buying any of his other toys had been. It was more satisfying than work.

Josh talked to one of the dishwashers he had worked with and got his brother's phone number. He was a mechanic. After some persuasion and a few hundred dollars, he secured himself some time in the shop. The restoration had progressed to the point where more serious tools were required.

The car was getting close to being finished. There had been some mishaps along the way and it would never be 100%, but Josh was proud of himself. He was sad to see it come to an end. It had been something to look forward to and a welcome distraction.

As the project wound down, it left room in his mind for Emily. They had not spoken since she walked out that night. If the last time they had spoken was any example, she wouldn't be the one to make the first move.

Emily wasn't the only thing creeping back into his mind. Try as he might, he couldn't lose himself in his work as he did before the car. The fact that there was more to life than work was more painfully obvious than ever. He didn't think he could deny it anymore and he was afraid.

Of course he wanted there to be more to his life than work. Deep down he wanted to do something he loved. And if he could just figure out what he loved, he'd do it.

At work he'd been hearing rumors that another promotion was in store for him. When his boss called him into his office, he wasn't surprised. He half-listened to his boss as he talked about how far he'd come and they were all glad that they had taken a chance on him.

"Congratulations."

Josh focused on his boss. He had come full circle and gotten nowhere he wanted to be. It was time to take another lap around.

"Aren't you happy?"

Josh stood up. "Sir, thank you, but I have to decline. Actually, I have to leave."

He walked back to his office, collected

his few things and headed for the lobby.

"Josh!"

He kept walking.

"Josh, where are you going?"

Slowing, he looked back. "I'm sorry. I've got to take a chance again."

"Josh!" his boss yelled exasperatedly.

He sped back up and walked out.

There was already a message on his machine when he got home. He ignored it, got changed, and walked out to the Mustang. He put the top down and headed for the highway. He stopped for gas and a snack and didn't stop again until almost midnight.

After putting the top up, he slid into the back seat and went to sleep.

Chapter 16

Rush hour traffic and the sun woke him early. At the first exit, he got off and looked for somewhere to get breakfast. Not finding the diner he was hoping for, he settled for a coffee shop breakfast sandwich. Then he headed home.

He asked for and got his dishwashing job back. He started riding his bike again. And he did, in fact, paint again.

With his first painting finished, he had a new goal. The next day he wrapped up his painting in brown paper and left it on Emily's doorstep.

After a week he hadn't heard anything. He wrapped up the second painting he had finished and left it for her.

This continued for two months before he came home to a message from her. She wanted to meet for coffee the next evening.

"Hello, Emily."

"Hi."

"How have you been?"

"Fine, and you? I see you've been painting again."

"I've been good. I'm dishwashing again. And, yes, painting. And riding my bike. And," he turned to the parking lot behind him, "I fixed up a car. The blue Mustang."

"Sounds like you're getting your life together. The car looks beautiful. I just wish you hadn't waited so long to get around to painting again. I'm… I'm seeing someone now."

"Oh. That's great. I'm glad you're happy."

"I'm sorry, Josh, But I didn't hear anything from you after I left that night."

"I am sorry about that. I needed to try that out. I wanted to know if that was what missing from my life."

"What did you find out?"

"It wasn't what I had hoped for. Rebuilding the car made me a lot happier. Maybe I'm suppose to be a mechanic," he laughed.

She smiled wanly at him. "Josh, I'm glad you're trying to figure things out, but I don't think cutting people out of your life is a good way to do it."

"I agree. That's why I wanted to talk to you again."

"Listen, I'm glad that you did. But it's not fair to do this to me. When I left, I thought that you would come after me. At the very least, I thought you would call the next day. When a week had passed, I began wondering if what we had meant anything to you. And after a month, I gave up.

"You hurt me a lot. I'm sorry that you're this lost and confused. But you can't keep taking it out on those of us who are going after something in life."

He stared sullenly at the table. She, as usual, was right. All he ever did was let people down. He let people into his life when it was convenient and he always let them down. His employers, Anna, Emily. Adelaide.

"Josh?"

Would he ever learn from his mistakes?

"Yes."

"You haven't said anything."

"I don't know what to say. You're right. That's all there is to say."

He just wanted to go to the beach and think for a while. They got up to leave and walked outside to find that it was raining. It was too chilly tonight to go sit on the seawall in the rain, so he went home.

Nick was in the kitchen when he got back. They didn't really speak anymore. He went to the living room and sat in his chair. This room used to make him happy. He had poured money into it. It was all so unnecessary. There was no substance, no character.

Everything he had done had been such a waste of time and effort. Nothing made him happy. He didn't make anyone happy. Everything had been so haphazard. Nothing ever worked. It never got any better. He was tired of screwing up. He was tired of trying.

It had been only a few months since he

had gotten back his dishwashing job, but they liked him enough to give him a few weeks off. He let Nick know he'd be gone for a little while and not to worry if he didn't see him in the next week.

This would probably take longer than the last time. He didn't ride as often or as far as he once had. He was older. But he was confident that he could still do it.

The panniers and pack had sat unused for a while. They were still in a box that he dug out of the basement. In that box was his notebook from the trip. He looked through his sketches of the coffee shop, the beach, the woods. He had been so excited and optimistic then.

He paused at a paragraph that described something he had read in one of his Buddhist books, how contemplation of beauty eliminated desire, being happy in just seeing something beautiful and not needing to have it. In his writings he had been convinced that this was part of the path to happiness and that he was on his way. Despite all his efforts over the years, he had lost that optimism, that sense of being able to happily make his way through the world.

This life he lived now was what he had tried to escape. It was routine and unexciting. There was a lack of passion and dedication. The previous week while he was shaving, he looked at himself in the mirror and saw in his eyes the deadened look he had tried so hard to fight off. He wouldn't look in his eyes anymore. This time he didn't have any plan to make it go away. All he could do was hope that this might keep it from getting worse and spreading.

The first day he stopped by the seawall before leaving. The sun was just edging over the horizon. The clouds made golden slashes across the sky. He filled his lungs with the salty air. Content, he took one last look at the sea and set off toward the main road through town.

After two hours, he passed into unfamiliar territory. Occasionally he would see things that he had passed on the first trip. Most of the landscape was new, having been built up over the years. This route had been flanked by trees the last time, but there was now a proliferation of subdivisions and strip malls.

He made it thirty miles before calling it a day. It was a respectable distance, but well shy of a typical day on the first attempt. Nor was he as inclined to sleep under trees in a tent. He stopped at the first motel he found, got a first floor room, and collapsed on the bed.

A large fluorescent light fixture lit the room in a yellowish hue. The thin walls made the TV in the next room sound like it was next to him. Unable to sleep and his stomach reminding him that it hadn't been fed in several hours, he took a shower and rode downtown.

The café he found was quiet. The service was slow and the waitress was disgruntled. What had ever possessed him to give up his life as he knew it for a waitress he didn't even know? Adelaide. She had caused him nothing but problems. He had been so desperate for an answer then that he leapt at the first thing that came close. Who knows what he had missed for the rest of that trip? This time he would do better.

At the motel, the sound of the TV had been replaced by snoring. Exhausted, he turned the light off and fell asleep shortly.

He slept until 10 the next day. His back ached and his legs were sore. It would be a short day. He followed the same road out of town as he had many years before. He was certain of what he would find if he stuck to this route.

Seven hours later, it was there. The restaurant. He was suddenly very nervous. What would he say to her if she was there? What was he hoping for? And what if she wasn't there? Nine years was a long time to work at a sleepy, small-town diner.

There was a young girl working, no older than 18, and a cook with his back to the counter. Relief and sadness took a hold.

He slowly ate his grilled cheese and minestrone soup. The soup was cold by the last spoonful and the excess cheese had congealed to the plate. Not being able to justify staying any longer, he paid the check and went to find somewhere to sleep that night.

The next morning he woke up at seven and went back to the diner. A different girl was working, but it wasn't Adelaide. For the next four days he took all his meals there.

After his final meal there, he returned to his motel room. It had been foolish to think that after all this time she would still be working there. Without a name, he would never find her. Hollowness filled his core. So badly he wanted to know where she was, if she was happy, if she was still contentedly waiting tables. This trip had really been about finding that out. If he had only gotten her name. Someone at the diner would be bound to know who she was.

He sat on the edge of the bed and stared at the salmon colored wall. This wasn't how his life was supposed to turn out. There was nothing of substance in his life. Desperate loneliness filled his life. All he had ever wanted was to be happy. Or even reasonably satisfied. The people who came in and out of his life all seemed to have found that. For all his efforts, he felt further from it than when he started.

Josh lay back on the bed. A hint of stale cigarette smoke clung to thin maroon floral-print comforter. He searched so hard for purpose and never found it. Somehow his life had led him to this point without one. Perhaps fate had passed him over by accident and this was all there was. This is all there would ever be.

He fell asleep turning this over in his head. He awoke after four in the morning. His legs, draped over the edge of the bed, had both fallen asleep. Trying not to move them as they pricked painfully, he slid back to rest his head on the pillows.

For the next hour he traced the edges of the watermarks on the ceiling with his eyes. When the glow of the streetlights disappeared from the edge of the curtains, he rose.

He gathered his things back into his pack and left cash and the key on the dresser.

Chapter 17

Out of habit, he locked his bike to the snow fence separating the dunes from the parking lot. He took one thing from the pack and left the rest on the ground. He picked up one thing from the foot of the fence and walked along the boardwalk towards the water.

As the new day broke and the sky flamed red, a verse he learned in childhood ran through his head.

Red sky in morning,
Sailors take warning
Red sky at night,
Sailors delight

As he hefted the cinderblock tied to his waist toward the ocean, he wondered what about the sky at daybreak over the ocean had always fascinated him so. He took some comfort in the fact that he would now become one with it, that he could spend his last moments as part of the endless sea. The endless cycle of tides, the circle of life and death played out in its depths, the ever changing but always constant waters would be a part of him.

Despite the humid August air, the water numbed his feet quickly. He relished the burning and kept going. As the water reached his shoulders and the waves nicked his chin, Josh paused to take one last look at the empty beach and then at the sun, now fully emerged from the horizon. Satisfied, he took a deep breath and walked until he couldn't hold it in any longer.

He let the block drop.

And as if to torment him once again, the last thing he saw in his mind was Adelaide.

But she wasn't there to torment him.

The tension around his waist slackened and he floated up. Instinct kicked in and he gasped for air as he broke the surface. Adelaide was treading water next to him. Deciding he would live, she swam back towards shore.

He watched her swim away. Realizing he had no idea what to do now, he followed her to shore.

They stood on the sand facing each other.

"What, no thank you?"

He just kept staring. It was *Adelaide*. It couldn't really be her. He must be dead. Maybe this is how a person crossed over to the afterlife.

"That was a pretty creative way to go. I thought you were just drowning at first." She flashed a knife at him. "Lucky for you, I always carry this. A girl's got to be able to protect herself, you know."

"Are you really Adelaide?"

"Adelaide? No. That's a funny name.

I'm Jenny."

"Oh, right. I never knew your name."

"Have we met before?"

"Not really. You were my waitress a few years back."

"Really? That was a long time ago that I did that. It's been nearly 10 years since I quit it."

"But you seemed happy doing it."

She gave him an amused smile. "Well, yeah, but not for the rest of my life. I decided to do something more. I'm a yoga instructor now."

"Oh."

"Hey, why do you remember a waitress from 10 years ago? Did you think I was hot or something?" she teased.

"It's a long story." He was getting a bit flustered.

"Well, I figure since I just saved your life, you owe me a good story at least."

With an embarrassed smile, he agreed.

"Not now. I need to finish my run. You can buy me dinner tonight and tell me then." She glanced around and gestured back to the dunes. "Meet me in the parking lot at 6, ok?"

He nodded and she turned and jogged a few paces.

She stopped and called back, "You'll be ok now, right? No more swimming?"

"No more swimming."

Satisfied, she continued on down the

beach.

He sat in the sand and watched the sun finish rising. She was beautiful. And happy.

He checked into a nearby motel and rinsed the salt and sand from himself. There were seven more hours before he was to meet her. He rode into town and meandered down the stretch of shops.

He had almost a week of vacation time left. He had planned on biking back, but now that he had found Adelaide, he wanted to stay as long as he could.

Her mix of confidence, playfulness, and determination was refreshing. As he got to know her, it quickly became apparent to him what he lacked. Each day that week, they would meet for dinner at one of the restaurants along the waterfront and then go sit on the beach. This quickly became the highlight of his day. There was a deep and powerful satisfaction in this simple routine. And for the last six days he was there, he wanted to describe himself as happy.

On the day before he was to leave, he spent the hours before he met Jenny contemplating where to go from here. There wasn't much waiting for him at home. The only responsibility he had there was his job and he was ambivalent about that.

On a whim, he took a ride around to get a feel for the area. There were four houses for sale around the downtown area, but they were all small and boxed in by their neighbors. He rode further out from town and the houses became further and further spaced apart. He passed a few lots of land for sale and one dilapidated house. Finally he noticed a familiar angularly marked blue and white sign down the road. It sat in front of what appeared to be a sizeable property.

It was a low, sprawling farmhouse. A gravel driveway led up to the side door and made an abrupt right there to continue on to a small barn. It was nothing spectacular to behold and the word "ramshackle" came in and out of his mind as he looked it over. But he wanted it. Even as he let his mind run with the possibilities of living there, another part of him hesitated. Should he really up and leave again and start over? Here he would know nothing but the brief glimpses of the town he had seen on his two visits and Jenny.

After jotting down the name and number of the realtor, he rode back to the motel to get ready for dinner.

He and Jenny sat in the restaurant for over 3 hours, lingering in each other's presence. It grew near closing time and the waitress kept walking by, giving them impatient glances. They finally parted after exchanging phone numbers.

On the flight home he thought of her. She made him feel alive. That had to be worth something. It had to be worth taking a chance on.

He hadn't mentioned the farm or anything else to her. He didn't want to get her hopes up or scare her off.

It surprised him how easily he could see himself moving and farming and living on his own and doing his art.

Once back home he called the realtor and found out the asking price. After looking over his mortgage bill, he realized that he'd be pretty well off financially if he did what he wanted. Over the years he had been paying a little extra every month and it had added up.

Last time he gave everything up, though, it hadn't fixed a thing. Discontentment still roiled under the surface. It was a different set of circumstances, but the same life. The same justifications ran through his head—if he didn't change now, when would he? How could he change by going through the same motions every day? The peace he sought seemed to still be attainable, just slightly beyond his grasp.

And so he began again. The house went up for sale and an offer was put in on the farm. There wasn't as much to do this time—he had never really built a life here.

Within the month everything had been wrapped up and he had begun the drive down.

He had not seen the farm since he left the beach and had never seen the inside. He didn't know if the barn was structurally sound or where the property ended. He was going into it blind and knew that if he had told anyone his plans they would have thought him crazy. But it was a fresh start. There were no memories to overcome with this house, no past to attempt to right.

It was hot and muggy when he arrived. He dragged his mattress in and a few essentials and left them in the entryway. The power hadn't been turned on yet, but there was just enough light left to take a quick tour of the house and yard. It was an old building and the inside was coated with many whitewashed layers of paint. It seemed to be a sound home overall. Tired from the drive, he left his mattress in the entryway and fell asleep there.

Daylight streaming through the bare windows woke him early. He went to the back porch to watch day break. As the air warmed, steam rose up from the field, creating a lazily swirling mist.

Once the rising sun had burned off the last remnants, he got his bike and rode into town. Inside his chest he felt a new lightness. The deep purple cumulus clouds on the horizon made him smile, the car with children trailing paper fish on string out the window in the wind made him smile, the cheerful weekend people at the coffee shop he stopped at made him smile.

He rode down to the beach with his o.j.

and doughnuts and watched the clouds blown out over the water from behind him. The line of dark water pushed the blue further and further out as the clouds moved toward the horizon. The breeze picked up and whitecaps sprung up. Knowing a downpour was imminent, he gulped down the last sip of o.j. and walked his bike back to the pavement. He had wanted to call Jenny, but decided it was probably better if he unpacked.

He unloaded the trailer he had rented. What he did have didn't fill the house, but he wasn't concerned. The thought of having empty space surrounding him brought him an odd contentment. He chose the largest upstairs room as his bedroom, dragged his mattress into a corner and set up his dresser. This would be good enough for now. He brought his art supplies into the barn. It was ramshackle, at best. There was no power that he could see and it needed a good cleaning. It looked like animals of some sort had taken up residence in once corner and the birds were enjoying the rafters. After a brief survey, he set off into town to return the trailer and pick up supplies.

For the next few days, he assessed the state of the farm, unpacked, and left only for food and supplies to do work on the house. A rhythm developed of waking with the sun, watching it rise, and then beginning his day.

The barn was the focal point of his

efforts. He built benches and a work table and cabinets and drawers for his painting supplies. He fixed the siding and patched the visible damage on the roof and waited for the next rain to test the results of his handiwork. When everything proved watertight, he moved all of his art supplies out there.

He painted the kitchen and figured out what crops he could plant next year. He had about 5 acres to work with and decided to start off planting one acre with corn, tomatoes, squash, cucumbers, green beans, beans, and watermelon. He doubted the greenness of his thumb, but figured something would grow out of all of that.

This went on for the better part of a month. As the amount of necessary work tapered off, he found a tinge of loneliness creeping in.

He got another dishwashing job, at the one of the restaurants where he and Jenny had eaten, and started painting more. After work one day, he ventured to call Jenny. It had been nearly 3 months since they had last spoken.

"Who did you say this was?"

"Josh. You pulled me out of the ocean a few months back."

"Josh! How are you? I tried calling you once, but your phone had been disconnected."

"Oh, yeah. I moved."

"Where to?"

"Hey, do you want to meet up for

dinner? We can catch up on everything."

"You're in the area again?"

"Yeah, I am."

"Sure then, why not?"

They met at the same restaurant they first had dinner at. It was also where Josh now worked.

"I was beginning to think I had scared you off."

"It would be pretty hard for you to do that. I just got busy with moving stuff. But what have you been up to?"

"Same stuff—teaching yoga, running on the beach, dragging the occasional lost soul out of the ocean." She grinned slyly at him.

He smiled back at her. "Nothing new going on?"

"I did meet this guy while I was jogging one morning, but I'm not sure where that's going yet. I won't bore you with the details, though. What about you? What's new with you? Where'd you move to?"

He tried not to let his disappointment show as he answered. "Not much new going on aside from moving. I moved to a nice farm with a barn and everything."

"Whereabouts?"

He held her gaze for a moment before answering. "About 3 miles west of here."

They stared at each other.

She looked away and picked at her

napkin.

"When did you do this?"

"A couple of months ago. I've been getting settled in and working."

Jenny started to say something, but stopped. She studied his face.

"Did you move here for me?" There was a hard edge in her voice.

He hesitated before answering, not wanting to tell her the truth. She wouldn't understand.

"I liked the area a lot when I visited. I was out for a ride and saw this farm for sale and fell in love with it. It has a huge barn where I can do my art and it's still close to the ocean. I admit that I thought of you in making my final decision. It was nice to know that I'd at least know one person here if I did move."

There was suspicion in her eyes. "You said you got a job down here. What are you doing?"

"Dishwashing again."

The suspicion changed to anger. "What's wrong with you? You try killing yourself, disappear, then move down here, get a dishwashing job, and then randomly call and invite me here. Do you think that's normal? Who does that?" She was leaning forward and glaring at him. "I think it's a little messed up."

"I told you, I liked it down here. I found a house I liked. I got a job dishwashing because it was something familiar in a place where I don't know my way around just yet."

The rest of the meal passed in mostly silence and terse sentences. Back at home that evening that familiar discomfort floated around in the back of his head. He suspected that he had repeated his mistakes again. Another move, another upheaval, another lost girl, another failure.

He sat on the back porch and watched the fireflies flicker in and out of the treetops. It was beautiful here. He hadn't seen this many fireflies in his life before moving here. There was a serenity in the cooling night air, a sweetness in the smell of it. Away from town, the stars were bright and easy to see.

Sometimes he couldn't decide if he liked the smell of this or the salty ocean air better. But the ocean was in his blood and it always edged out the sweet summer air. Despite the peacefulness, there was a deep sadness in his chest. It was in moments like this, where everything seemed good and beautiful, that he was most naked with the world. It was when he was forced to deal with his actions and his consequences and the state of his life. There were none of his familiar constructs and walls protecting him from it now.

Each time he moved, he expected his problems to be fixed. Each new job and each new relationship were supposed to provide him with the answers. Each purchase he made and each painting he painted were supposed to smooth over and erase the hurt. It was a vain hope that propelled him forward, but disappointed him every time.

They were all just temporary anesthetics. He couldn't figure out what the permanent solution was. He had a sense of gradually spiraling downward, edging further and further away from where he was supposed to be with each turn. The intense frustration of not being able to find an answer made him want to tear himself asunder, limb by limb, screaming. It churned in his chest and he wanted to rip it out and stomp it to death. He kept it well hidden most of the time, but when he couldn't, it tormented him.

Years ago he hadn't worried about it so much. He was young and figured he had many years ahead of him to make mistakes and sort it all out. Now, as he hovered around middle age, he knew that wasn't the case. He didn't have much to show for himself. He lacked commitment, hopping from one thing to the next. How had he ever made it through school before? No longer could he imagine devoting four years to anything.

Chapter 18

At night he would lay and listen to the white noise of the nocturnal insects. Sometimes, the long blare of a train horn would cut through. When he first moved in, the noise would rouse him from slumber throughout the night. Now, the sound comforted him. There was a security in the continuity throughout the years of trains crossing the country. Despite all the technological progression, trains still couldn't be surpassed for the shipping of some cargos. Every night, he could count on the insects and trains.

Chapter 19

A block more and he'd be at the yoga studio. He wasn't sure how'd she react to seeing him again. The last time hadn't gone so well. It was two weeks later and he hoped she had calmed down. His stomach clenched, partly with nervousness about how she'd react and partially with disappointment in himself for waiting so long to begin with and possibly having lost her.

Locking his bike to a sign post, he began walking over. Just out of view of the front window, he waited. He stared in the direction of the water. Only a narrow view of it was afforded through the gap between the buildings across the street. Calmness spread through him. Sighing, he turned to walk in.

Jenny was 6 inches from him as he turned around.

He stepped back. "Hey."

"Have you been standing here long?"

"No, no. Just a minute. I was- I wanted to see you and talk things over." He took a deep breath, trying to calm himself again.

"I'm about to go get lunch. You can come with me, if you want."

"Ok."

She walked down to the restaurant where they first had dinner and where he now worked.

The hostess greeted him, "Hey Josh. What are you doing here?"

Jenny stared at him.

"Just getting some lunch."

"Sure thing. Feel free to sit anywhere."

Josh walked over to a table in a corner and avoided looking at Jenny.

She said nothing at first and finally said, "Why does she know you?"

He suspected that she already knew the answer. "I work here."

"For how long?"

"Two months or so."

"You've been working a couple blocks from where I work for two months and you never came by to say hi or even let me know you were in town?"

He fidgeted with his napkin. At this point, it might be better just to give up on her, he thought. Everything since he had seen her again had been horrible. The chances of recapturing anything they had before he left were getting smaller and smaller. He suspected that again he had messed everything up.

He decided honesty might be his best choice. "I didn't call you or come see you right away because I didn't want to scare you off. I wasn't sure how'd you react if you knew that I had moved down here. I didn't move just for you, but you were a large part of it. I like you a lot. When I got here, I wanted to settle in and give you some time and space before I sprung this on you. But I screwed up and I let too much time go by. And the more time that passed, the less I knew what to say to you. Then I saw you the other week and figured then was as good a time as any to finally break the ice. I'm dumb. I'm impulsive. I get scared off easily. None of these ever work in my favor. And that's where things are now."

She looked fixedly out the window. She scanned the faces of people passing by for a few minutes and turned back to him.

"Josh, I'm not seeing anyone. I said that because I was angry with you for falling off the face of the earth. I like you too, but I'm worried you're going to hurt me. I have no reason to think you won't, given your actions since we've met. I'm scared that if I even attempt to see where things with you go, I'll wake up one morning and you'll have disappeared again. And why shouldn't I worry about that? You've done it before!" Her eyes flashed and he stayed silent. "Did you think you'd move here and things would just be great and everything would be fine?"

"Sorta. I was hoping, anyhow. I know it wasn't realistic, but that's what ideally would have happened. Things were pretty good last time I was here."

"You're an asshole, Josh. A naive asshole. And I really wish I didn't like you."

Chapter 20

The sun illuminating the inside of his eyelids a glowing red prompted him to awaken. He rolled over and looked at Jenny as the light tickled her face. For a brief moment, he was brought back to those days that he had watched the sun play over Anna's face until it woke her. The circumstances of his life were so different now, but the underlying current was the same.

Jenny had given him another chance, though he didn't deserve it. The past few months with her had been better than he could have expected, but there was a dark undercurrent he couldn't quite put his finger on.

If he had to guess, he would have said it was the knowledge of being responsible if things went downhill. She decided to let him into her life again and take a chance and he was terrified that he would ruin it all again. That was the pattern of his life--taking good things and ripping them down, like the bully on the playground who just couldn't seem to bear anyone building anything good. It was never malice that prompted him to do this, just a desire for a perfection that could never be real.

She opened her eyes and saw him

watching her. A smile played across her lips as she gently shoved him away. "Have you been watching me sleep? You know I think it's creepy when you do that."

"And you know I can't help it. You're amazingly beautiful in the morning light." He paused, thinking over his words. "Of course you're always beautiful, which is why it's amazing that you can be even more beautiful." He reflected on this, realized it wasn't quite right either and started to speak again, but she stopped him. "Cut your losses now, buddy, before you dig yourself into too deep a hole."

It turned out that in addition to everything else, Jenny had a bit of a green thumb. As winter let up its grip she told him when things needed to be planted. Brussel sprouts first. Then a few weeks later the tomatoes. She showed him how to build a cold frame so that he could get the seeds started earlier and bought him a couple books on basic gardening and a planting schedule for the area.

It was peaceful. In the monotony and rituals of planting and weeding he found a satisfaction, similar to when he had worked on the car. Each day he would go out to check the progress, marveling as shoots emerged from the earth, cheering the fledgling plants on after he transplanted them, and finally being amazed as things he could eat began to show themselves and ripen.

The weather became a friend and

nemesis as he hoped for sun, but not too much heat; rain, but not downpours. He began to formulate plans for the next year and how he could do better. Starting to compost now to create good soil, adding a rain barrel so he could always have good water. He considered adding a few chickens for the eggs and the manure, goats to keep the scrub from overtaking the acres he wasn't using yet.

The growing season drew to a close as the nights grew gradually colder and the first frost hit. Jenny had moved in and they made plans to improve the house. He had been in town for just over a year and hadn't done much to the place after his initial improvements. The house was still sparsely furnished even with the addition of Jenny's belongings and it was still stuck in another era. There was much to do and it would keep his hands busy when the garden couldn't. He contemplated painting again, but it had largely fallen by the wayside once he and Jenny had picked things up. She had been hinting at improvements to the house and he was happy to have those take priority.

They got started in the bedroom, taking down the long-faded wallpaper. The old plaster walls needed some patching, but were in pretty good shape considering their many decades of service. The project took most of the day and then they were ready to move on to priming and painting.

At the hardware store they discussed paint colors. Jenny paused mid-sentence while discussing the pros and cons of a handful of samples and smiled at him. "This is our first real joint decision. About our home or our lives."

He smiled back, pondering the "our" that was now in her vocabulary. There had never been much "our" in his. It was his house and his job and his bike riding and his unhappiness and his search for meaning, always at the expense of all others. Now it was "our." A paint color that was "ours." A house that was "ours." He was supposed to be responsible for more than himself now. If he left, he would be leaving his house. "Our" house. Or leave her in it, though everything was in his name.

This was how things were supposed to be, right? Growing up, buying a house, falling in love, making joint decisions? He had always been fine with all of those things, except for the last. With Anna, with Emily, major decisions were his. He would leave, he would quit his job, he would disappear. If they were lucky, he'd tell them before he did it. Somehow, "our" felt a little better with Jenny, but it also triggered a deep-seated fear.

They settled on a soft mossy green, gathered brushes and rollers and trays, dropclothes, and a 5 gallon bucket of primer, and went home to paint. As the walls whitened, hiding the parchment colored plaster, the room did feel more and more like it was really theirs, less like he was squatting in an abandoned farmhouse. It was well after midnight when the last yellowish spot changed to white. Exhausted, they left everything where it was, removed their paint splattered clothes, and collapsed on the mattress, which had been dragged into the hall to keep it clean.

Josh awoke before her and surveyed the damage. Her hair was flecked in white spots, splattered there from the roller. The tips of her fingers, poking out from her head that rested on her hand, were smeared white. Some of the paint must have still been wet when she lay down and there were streaks of white on the pillowcase. Rolling over, he assessed his pillow and saw the same.

He sank back down into his pillow, smiling, watching her sleep. Our mess. Gently, he rose and walked into the bedroom. The early sun filled the room with soft white light and he sat down in the middle of the room, gazing out the window at sun trickling through the leaves of a nearby tree.

There was a soft rustle behind him then her hands were on his shoulders. One hand came up and played through his hair.

"It's starting to feel a lot more homey already." He smiled as she said this, reaching his hand across to clasp the hand still on his shoulder.

"Let's eat and then get this finished so we can set this up as a proper bedroom finally."

They rode bikes down to the restaurant where he worked. He had found a free one and fixed it up for her and she had started riding with him more and more. It was sometimes a little harrowing going down their narrow road that cars would speed down. Josh suspected she was growing to like the adrenaline of it.

"Hi, Josh."

"Hi, Irene."

"Go ahead and have a seat wherever you two want."

They sat in a booth by the window and he sat so he could look out towards the beach.

"It's been an interesting journey since the first time we met, hasn't it?"

He gave her a half grin. "At least I've stayed dry since then."

"From me dragging you out of the water to you moving down here and buying a house to me moving in and to now--us making the house ours. It's been a pretty crazy trip.

He nodded, not sure if this was just chit-chat or going somewhere.

"We seem to be getting pretty settled, but are you happy? Is this how you envisioned things?" She seemed a little wary asking this, like she was surprised that he had stuck around this long and not bolted as he seemed wont to do.

Josh looked to the beach, the grey sky spotted with lighter grey patches of clouds. The beach grass bent down in the breeze, then straightened back up as it relented. It would be raining soon.

It had been about a year and a half since Jenny had saved him from himself. He wanted to be happy, but mostly he had stopped thinking about it. It always seemed just out of reach. Keeping busy, occupying his time with work, fixing the house, gardening, those things kept the thoughts more comfortably hidden away. The day to day was easier that way. He spent less time in his head and more time in the physical world away from the endless self-doubt and knowledge that he was continuing to fail himself. The physical lended itself to small successes and easily correctable failures.

And then there was Jenny. There were a dozen small joys each day with her. A laugh, a smile, the way the sun caught her hair. Just sitting next to her on the couch as she was lost in a book.

But despite these ways he had learned to cope, the feelings that had always plagued him were always there.

She was still looking at him expectantly.

Panic crept up. Honesty around questions like these didn't usually go in his favor. So he told her what he had been thinking, about the comfort in fixing the house and gardening and the joy that she brought into his life every day. The parts about the lingering unhappiness and knowledge that hadn't been dealt with he chose to edit out. It was mostly honest.

She took his hand and gazed contentedly at him. "Ok."

As they rode back to the house, rain soaking them through, his thoughts were in turmoil. He wished she hadn't brought up his happiness. Perhaps it was just that people never were truly happy. Were his expectations too high? Was it that his routine of fixing and building and loving her was the best that anyone could hope for?

They dried off, put on painting clothes, and tackled the first coat of green. Despite his painting skills as an artist, this kind of painting was not his forte. Green blobs materialized on the ceiling as he rolled too high. Jenny kept a watchful eye on him and wiped them off as they appeared. Lost in his thoughts, he didn't notice this at first. Finally, he turned to get more paint and she was standing close enough that his shoulder brushed her as he pivoted.

"Hi." She gave him a lopsided grin. "I was wondering when you might notice how messy you've been. What's going on in there?" she asked, gesturing with her green spotted rag at his head.

"Are people every truly happy? Like every day happy?" His brow furrowed.

"Of course not. That would be a

ridiculous standard. And if you were happy every day that would just become normal and "happy" wouldn't really have much meaning. There's more balance to life than that." She looked at him with a faintly puzzled expression. "You know that, right?"

On a level he did. But that nagging feeling that something was missing wouldn't leave him. That didn't seem normal. "I know." The rain had picked up outside, along with the wind. The hard crackling of leaves skating across the ground while being pummeled with the rain distracted him for a moment. That was concrete and real. His thoughts were a jumbled mess of right and wrong and do and should and can't and happy and miserable and escape. Endless searching for an answer that wasn't forthcoming. "Sometimes I get a little lost in my head."

"I think you should come to one of my yoga classes. It might help you feel a little more grounded."

Having no reason to say no, he agreed and they went back to painting and her wiping off his distracted roller marks.

Chapter 21

In his chest was a deep feeling of dread and that he could do no right. It was a darkness that made him want to apologize again and again and lower his head in shame. Jenny was upset with him again and again he couldn't find the words to properly explain what he meant. As he tried, it was like she didn't hear him and she got more upset and he got more frustrated. This would either end with yelling or him not speaking and walking off. No matter what, he would feel an impotent helplessness. Run. That was all he could think. He could go, be on his own, and he wouldn't feel like this anymore. Just sell the house. Go. End up where ever he may. Leave again when he felt like it. Paint again.

"Josh!"

He looked over towards her.

"You weren't even listening!"

Rising, he looked away and walked out the side door. He looked around the yard in detail, noticing the lawn needed mowing and the garden could use some weeding. The weeds started coming out, one by one, and his frustration slowly subsided. Leaving would fix one set of problems, but it wouldn't really make anything better. Jenny was supposed to be it. His happiness. If he couldn't make this work, there didn't seem to be much hope for anything else working. Did he really want to start again? Again? It would be a reaction to a symptom, not the cause. There had to be something wrong with him that was the cause.

After another 20 minutes of pulling weeds he was ready to head back in. She was upstairs, taking a bath.

"Feeling better?" she inquired, with the slightest hint of sarcasm. It got under his skin, but he didn't have the energy to argue again.

"Yes." He paused to collect his thoughts. "I hate fighting with you. I don't really know how to and the only response I know is to leave."

"Like you've always left." She was needling him and clearly not done fighting.

"Yes, like I've always left. Because it's all I know. And just because it's all I know doesn't mean I think it's right. But I've never really learned anything else."

"What do you want, Josh? Just to not fight and pretend everything is fine? Do you really think there's a magical place where there's no discord and discomfort? Because if you do, you're in for a lot of disappointment in your life. And I honestly don't know how you've made it this far in life with the coping mechanisms you have. Though I guess you haven't really made it that far. You're pushing 40 and still a dishwasher, for Christ's sake."

"All I want is to be happy. And nothing

seems to work."

"Are you saying we're not working? Because you have to work at us for this to work. Unless you want to just delude yourself into thinking things are ok when they're not." She looked out the window and stared out, looking up at the afternoon sun playing through the beautiful explosion of fall leaves. This was usually the happiest time of year, the time when everything seemed possible, but instead it just served as a harbinger of the dark and cold that was right around the corner. She looked back at him, no longer trying to get under his skin. "I think you should talk to someone."

"Like a shrink?"

"Yeah. You're looking for something that you're not going to find without seriously shifting your view of things. We just keep fighting. I think you need to bring in someone else who doesn't have a vested interest."

He looked down, picking the dirt from weeding out of his fingernails as he thought about this. It was admitting a level of weakness, but he didn't have much else to lose. "Ok."

Twice a week he now rode his bike into town to meet with Dr. Richards. She had suggested this frequency after the first session. It made him feel more broken to need to see her this much, but he lacked the energy to defend himself. And she was the expert.

"It seems like you've spent your life running, Josh. From your parents to your jobs to your relationships to your responsibilities, you've left when you've thought there might be something better. How has that worked out for you?"

He looked down as he answered. "It's always better at first. A new adventure, new things to learn and see. Whatever was bothering me before I left is gone. It's good for awhile, then it gets boring or hard or both and it's time to move on again."

"So you feel like this strategy has served you well and is one that you'd like to continue?"

"What other options do I have? Everything only provides temporary happiness."

"Have you considered that perhaps you are looking for happiness in the wrong kinds of things?"

"It's not like I'm a drunk or a drug addict. Is it really that bad to want to be happy in a relationship or a job or with a house? It seems like those are pretty healthy things."

"And they are. But it seems that you are relying on those things to be your sole source of happiness. It is inevitable that they won't make you happy every day. They may bring you satisfaction on a day to day basis, but expecting happiness will lead to disappointment. If you were happy all the time, that would become normal. And it wouldn't make you happy. There needs to be a balance of good and bad so that you appreciate the good."

She had his full attention now. Jenny had said the same thing to him. Had she been talking to Dr. Richards or was this some commonly known fact he managed to miss his whole life?

"I leave though because I can't find any more good. So I leave to go find it."

"Are you religious?"

Strange question. He shook his head. "No. I was raised Catholic, but I left that a long time ago."

"Why'd you leave?"

"I didn't agree with what I was being taught. And I had stopped believing in God. I believe again now, but I'm not really one for organized religion."

"There are many types of religions, some much less formal than others."

"I know. I used to read a lot about different ones."

She had a slight glimmer in her eye. "I'm going to suggest that we not meet again for a week. And I'm going to give you a homework assignment. Read a book on religion. Any book, but try to have it be more of a personal experience than a history or explanation. Be prepared to talk about it next week and how it made you feel."

That was easy enough. He wondered if she thought he was getting better since she had given him a brief reprieve from meeting. "Ok, I can do that."

After leaving, he rode over to the library. It was close to where he worked, but it was his first time going. Many years ago now, the library had been his sanctuary. Thinking back, he remembered devouring books, searching for truth. That was what had led him to this place. That endless, impossible search for the one truth that didn't seem to exist, but tormented him as though just out of reach. Each book had seemed to bring him closer, but raised more questions. It had been so long since he read much of anything. Now older, maybe wiser, he'd be able to find better answers?

Walking through the front door felt like a homecoming. The familiar feel of the not quite bright enough lighting that seemed typical of all libraries, sunlight catching the dust drifting through the air, the hallowed stillness and soft rustling of pages.

Not knowing where any of the different subjects lived, he began shuffling slowly along rows, spot-checking titles to see if he was close. After pacing through 7 rows, he arrived. *The History of Saint Theresa of Avila Parish*, *The Art of Happiness*, *Gems of Wisdom from the Seventh Dalai Lama*. He ran his finger over the different titles, tilting some out towards him to see the cover. Pulling one from the shelf, he went to go sign up for his first library card in nearly a decade.

Back at home, he read. Jenny would occasionally come in to ask him a question or make a request, but his terse responses kept her at bay for several hours. *The Art of Happiness* was first on his list. It was what he was after, after all. Engrossed, time flew by. He devoured it. It all seemed so simple and easy. Anyone should be able to do this, be happy. Maybe this was all he needed. Some focus and direction and he could finally get himself out of his rut. He didn't need Jenny or the house or his art or his therapist to make him happy. Just himself.

After a few hours he wanted a break to let his mind process all that he had just read. He got his bike out of the barn and set off. Darkness surrounded him. It was a few miles from the shore, where most of the shops and activity was, and the stars were the brightest source of light at his property. He rode toward the light, looking forward to listening to the waves crash into the evening.

It had to all be simple--happiness. It didn't seem like others struggled like he did. Had he missed something in his childhood, in his formative years, that everyone else experienced that set them on the right path? Had he been on the outside all this time, an odd curiosity to those who had things figured out and watched as he turned in endless, useless circles?

Pedaling down the road in dark stillness, he felt a part of the world, but so separate from people. This was when he felt most at home. Himself in an ocean of solitude. It was a moment of perfection.

Headlights behind him pierced the darkness and illuminated his path. He slowed and rode carefully off the road into the dirt shoulder. The car slowed and passed, then accelerated quickly, leaving behind a faint cloud and stink of burning oil and the renewed expanse of black.

He could be happy in the moments where he was one person alone, dwarfed in the entirety of the world around him. It seemed like there must be some way to preserve this feeling to allow him happiness for more than a few moments. But eventually loneliness would creep in if this was all there was for too long. Not enough nature, too much nature. Too many people, too much loneliness. Perhaps this is what he had failed to learn, he thought to himself, the continual fluctuations of life, the continual search for knowledge and satisfaction. The journey was what remained, in its many forms. Things passing in and by. Lightness cutting through the dark, then dark returning, eventually yielding to light, repeating.

The glow ahead of him continued to

increase. It was only a few more minutes of a ride to the beach, but he turned around, returned home, and crawled into bed next to Jenny, his light cutting through the darkness.

The morning broke and found Josh curled up to Jenny, softly smiling. He kissed her temple and rolled out of bed. She had to be at work in an hour, but he still had a few more before his shift at the restaurant, so he started breakfast for her. She padded down the stairs as he transferred the first batch of pancakes to a plate and covered them.

"I was going to surprise you!" he exclaimed, feigning disappointment.

Finishing cooking, he piled pancakes onto two plates and carried them over to her at the table.

"What's the special occasion?" she asked. "You never cook real food."

"Just trying to show you how special I think you are."

She grimaced at him, then grinned.

The week between his therapy sessions passed and he kept reading. As he kept reading he began to feel something that had long been dormant. A light seemed to re-ignite in his chest. It burned with life and love and he felt like he could conquer the world. Jenny noticed that he seemed more cheerful. "Is therapy helping?"

"Reading is helping. I got too far away from what is real."

He felt better, but something nagged at him. Was the only thing that would keep him happy reading? How could he do something with what he was reading to make it more concrete? Would he eventually become numb to the words that were bringing him peace now?

Chapter 22

It had been a bright light in the darkness, but he also knew that darkness would overcome again soon. It had been a long time since he felt satisfied or connected to her. He would wake up next to her in the morning, roll over and hold her, be content for a few moments. Then...just the same disappointments and wishes for change. The same routine. The same wanting for something more. The same wondering if there was someone out there who would truly inspire and motivate him. Instead, everyday was ok. Fine. No problem.

He wanted to have an adventure again and start from scratch. He wanted to feel alive, not trapped in this all-consuming box he had constructed. There was a world out there that he wanted to see but he knew that the time had passed. This would be all he had to show for his life.

Chapter 23

He had tried so many things. Each time he felt he had finally figured it out. Each time he thought he had found the elusive piece that had been missing. He was always wrong. As he drove along the highway towards the river, he wondered what he could have done differently. Was there anything? Or was this simply how life is?

It didn't matter to him anymore, but he couldn't help but wonder. The river and bridge came into view ahead. Maybe he hadn't tried enough. He pressed the gas steadily downwards. He knew he wouldn't have changed anything, he simply wished he had not hurt all the people he had. Perhaps it would have been worth it had his pursuit not been in vain, but he had cast them aside and gained nothing from it. He switched into the left lane and accelerated a bit more. He had seen a lot and learned a lot though. He was glad that he had chosen early on to get out of the corporate world and see the real world.

The car's speed was approaching the end of the speedometer. He was curious as to how high it would go. It was no use dwelling, it was all past him now and there was no more time for apologies or seconds thoughts. The bridge stretched over the river, gap between asphalt and water widening as he approached the center. It had been a good run. He pulled the wheel to the right and the car responded, skidding slightly, pummeled through the guardrail and concrete barriers, and arched out over the river.